To all children with challenges—learning might be hard, but you have greatness in you! And always, to Stacey—HW

In memory of Paula Danziger— beloved friend, great writer, defender of children—LO

by Henry Winkler and Lin Oliver

HANK ZIPZER

the world's greatest underachiever

Help!
Somebody Get Me
Out of Fourth Grade!

Grosset & Dunlap

GROSSET & DUNLAP
An Imprint of Penguin Random House LLC, New York

Text copyright © 2004 by Henry Winkler and Lin Oliver Productions, Inc.
Cover illustration by Tim Heitz, copyright © 2013 by Penguin Random House LLC.
Interior illustrations copyright © 2004 by Penguin Random House LLC.
All rights reserved. Published by Grosset & Dunlap,
an imprint of Penguin Random House LLC, New York.
GROSSET & DUNLAP is a trademark of Penguin Random House LLC.
Printed in the USA.

Visit us online at www.penguinrandomhouse.com.

Library of Congress Control Number: 2004020579

Proprietary ISBN 9781101951972   10 9 8 7 6 5 4 3 2 1

Part of Boxed Set ISBN 9781101951996

CHAPTER 1

"**Students, there will be excitement** in the classroom today," my teacher Ms. Adolf said. "Can you feel it?"

I tried. Oh, boy, did I try. I even lifted my palms off the desk and stuck them straight out in the air to see if they would pick up the excitement vibration.

Nothing. I felt nothing.

I looked around to see if I could see anything unusual in the classroom. It looked like the same old fourth-grade room at PS 87 where I had spent the last eight months of my life. Same old pale green walls. Same old desks lined up in totally straight rows just like Ms. Adolf likes them. Same old bulletin boards displaying the compositions of the best students in the class. Oh, in case you're wondering, mine wasn't up there. Never has been and never will be. But,

1

hey, a guy can dream, can't he?

So what could Ms. Adolf be talking about? Excitement? In school? As far as I'm concerned, school and excitement just don't go together.

I flapped my arms around again, just to make sure I wasn't missing anything.

"Frankie," I whispered to my best friend Frankie Townsend, who sits across the aisle from me. "Are you feeling the excitement?"

"Zip, the only thing I'm feeling is the breeze coming out of your armpits," he answered. "What's with all the flapping?"

"Excuse me, Henry," Ms. Adolf suddenly cut in. I looked up. She was staring at me over the top of her gray-rimmed glasses. "You seem to be in the midst of a conversation. I hope I'm not disturbing you."

"Oh, we're almost finished, Ms. Adolf," I said. "We were just trying to feel the excitement that you said was in the room."

Everyone laughed. Correction. Everyone laughed but Ms. Adolf. She gave me that stare. You know, the "one more wisecrack and you're on your way to Principal Love's office" stare. She's good at that. In fact, I think she invented it.

"Mr. Zipzer," Ms. Adolf said, "I hope you're not trying to be funny, because if there's one thing that annoys me, it's funny children having fun."

Ms. Adolf walked over to my desk and stood so close that I could see a piece of lint on her gray skirt, the one she wears every single day to school. For a second, I was tempted to reach out and pick it off, the way my mom is always picking bits of lint and donut crumbs and other stuff off of my clothes. There's something about a little clump of lint that screams, "Somebody remove me, please!" My hand was just starting to reach out for Ms. Adolf's skirt when my brain woke up and shouted at me:

Hank Zipzer, get your hand back here right now. You don't pick lint from your fourth-grade teacher's skirt region. That's beyond icky.

Fortunately, I pulled my hand back just in time. Another trip to Principal Love's office avoided!

I wasn't trying to get in trouble in class, but I'm going to tell you the truth because I feel I can trust you. It does feel really good to make thirty-one kids laugh, all at the same time. And when you're doing that, you're usually doing something that's going to get you in trouble.

Actually, on that particular Tuesday, it was only thirty kids that I made laugh. There was one, Nick the Tick McKelty, who definitely did not laugh. That was no surprise, though. Nick McKelty only laughs at his own jokes, which by the way, are not funny and are really, really mean.

Like the other day, we were playing handball on the playground, and for no reason at all McKelty turned to Ryan Shimozato and said, "Hey, punk, you're so short you should play handball on the curb." Then he laughed and belted out so much bad breath that everybody on the court gagged and ran for cover.

"Henry, I recommend you close your mouth and open your ears," Ms. Adolf snarled as she walked back to the front of the room, "because what I'm about to say has particular significance to you."

"I'm all ears, Ms. Adolf," I said. And I was. I even stopped breathing for a minute so that there was nothing but wide-open space between her mouth and my eardrum.

"There will be no school this coming Friday," she announced without even cracking a smile.

"It will be a day off for all of you."

"That definitely rocks, Ms. Adolf," I shouted.

Whoops, I did it again. I was the only kid in class who had opened his big mouth. Everyone else had the good sense to just enjoy her announcement quietly. Not me. It's like the minute something comes into my brain, it just slides right out my mouth. I really have to have a mouth cork made. I wonder if they make them kid–mouth sized.

My other best friend, Ashley Wong, raised her hand.

"Are we starting summer vacation early?" she asked. Frankie and I gave her a high five for the question.

"Absolutely not, young lady," Ms. Adolf said. "Summer vacation is too long as it is. You fourth-graders have too much fun. There's no need for excess fun."

I don't even know how to comment on that, because I know you and I are thinking the same thing. Now I ask you: Is there any such thing as a summer vacation that is too long? Let's answer that together:

NOOOOOOOOOOOOOOOOOOOOOO!!!!!

"Who knows why there will be no school on Friday?" Ms. Adolf asked.

Heather Payne, who always knows the answers to everything, raised her hand and waved it in front of Ms. Adolf's face like she was trying to swat a fly off her nose.

"It's fourth-grade Parent-Teacher Conference Day," Heather said in her Little Miss Perfect voice.

"That's correct, Heather," Ms. Adolf said. "Good job remembering."

"It's easy to remember, because we have it marked on our master calendar at home," Heather said. "It's written on a square right between my dental X-ray appointment and my French horn lesson."

Ms. Adolf smiled. "It makes me feel very warm inside when I see such excellent organizational skills," she said.

My family's master calendar would definitely not make old Ms. Adolf feel all warm inside. That's because it lives in a drawer in the kitchen, buried underneath boxes of aluminum foil and waxed paper and plastic baggies. It used to be up on the kitchen wall at the beginning of the school year. My dad put it up with a yellow thumbtack. But whenever my mom would write on it, the thumbtack would fall out, and the calendar would flop onto the kitchen floor. Then our dog, Cheerio, would attack it and try to tear the pages off with his teeth, which is why our calendar now lives in a drawer.

"The purpose of these conferences is for me to go over your end-of-the-year evaluations with your parents," Ms. Adolf was saying. "I'm sending home sign-up slips for your parents. Have them pick a time slot. Please bring back the slips tomorrow."

Ms. Adolf picked up a stack of pink sign-up sheets from her desk and walked around the classroom, handing one to each student. "I'll be discussing your overall work with your parents," she explained as she walked, "which will determine whether you continue your educational journey into the fifth grade."

After she passed by my desk, Nick McKelty leaned over to me as far as he could without bumping his Neanderthal head into the back of mine.

"In case you're wondering, Zipperhead, your

evaluation is going to suck . . . as always."

I wanted to turn around and tell him to take his disgusting mouth and put it on a jet and send it to Outer Mongolia, but I had already blurted out once today, and I didn't want to be sent to Principal Love's office, so I fought the urge.

I felt McKelty's hot breath in my ear. It's a good thing it wasn't any closer to me, because his breath would have melted the eraser off the top of my pencil.

"Forget it, Hankie boy," he whispered. "You won't be seeing the fifth grade. Everyone knows you're being left back, sucker."

That did it. I spun around in my chair and stared into his snaggly teeth, which were pointing at me from every direction.

"You don't know what you're talking about, McKelty," I said. "What everyone really knows is that you're a liar."

Those are strong words, I know, but they're the truth. McKelty exaggerates everything. Just take the truth and multiply it by one hundred, and you have what Frankie, Ashley, and I call the McKelty Factor. Like he told us that he went to the opening Yankees game, and they asked him to throw out the first pitch, but he said no because he thought they should ask the mayor of New York instead of him. Nick McKelty, president of the fourth-grade Bad Personality Club, didn't want to hurt the mayor's feelings. Right.

"Hey, Zipperbutt, I happen to know something you don't know," McKelty whispered.

I tried to ignore what he said. I tried, but I didn't succeed. McKelty's words started to buzz around in my head like a swarm of bees.

It's amazing to me how one kid can make you so mad. Who was he, Nick the Tick McKelty, to tell me that I was being left back in the fourth grade?

He doesn't know anything. That can't be right. Of course not.

Wait a minute. He might be right. I mean, I did get four Ds on my report card. And I still can't spell. And math . . . well . . . enough said about that. I don't even know my right from my left.

Oh, no! I'll bet he is right.

I'm going to be the only kid in my class repeating the fourth grade. That means I'm going to be in the same grade as my sister and her geeky, fact-spewing, nose-blowing, allergic-to-chocolate-cake boyfriend, Robert Upchurch.

This can't be happening to me.

I exploded out of my chair, my hand shooting up into the air.

"Ms. Adolf," I shouted before she even called on me. "Can I go to the library?"

"The library? You?"

"I have to find out how to dig a hole deep enough so that I can crawl into it and never be seen again!"

CHAPTER 2

Usually when the recess bell rings, Frankie and I are the first ones out of class and in line for tetherball. Frankie's the tetherball champ of PS 87. No kidding. When they put tetherball into the Olympics, Frankie Townsend will get the gold medal, for sure. And while we're discussing the Olympics, can anyone tell me why tetherball isn't an Olympic sport and synchronized swimming is? Girls in nose plugs? Give me a break. They should give *us* a gold medal for watching *them*!

Don't tell anybody about this, but I once tried synchronized swimming in my bathtub. I put my legs up high in the air, lost my balance, fell over, and caused a tidal wave so big that it flooded the bathroom. There was so much water on the floor and so few towels that I panicked. I jumped out of the tub and watched in horror as the water flowed under the door and into our hallway. I flung open the door and bolted for the linen closet to get more towels. As I grabbed a stack of towels and headed for the bathroom, I ran smack into my nine-year-old sister, Emily. Towels flew everywhere. I was totally naked, and she was totally screaming at the top of her lungs, which made me scream at the top of mine.

That little scream fest made our dachshund, Cheerio, start spinning in circles, which he does when he gets really nervous. As he spun right by me, I tripped over him and went sliding down the linoleum hall like a bowling ball, stopping just in time to wave hello to my mom, who was doing the dinner dishes.

"Hank, why are you sliding around naked?" my mom said.

"Just practicing my synchronized swimming, Mom. Gotta go."

Wait a minute. Where was I? Oh, yeah, I was telling you about how I like to be first in line for tetherball. I lose focus sometimes. Your mind wanders a lot when you have learning challenges like I do. My dad always says, "Stay focused." Hey, that's not as easy as it sounds.

The point here is that when the recess bell rang, I couldn't bolt out of my chair for the playground like I usually do. My legs felt like each one weighed about a thousand pounds.

"Let's jet," Frankie said to me. "What are you waiting for?"

"I have more important things than tetherball on my mind," I answered.

"What could be more important than that?"

"Being left back," I said. The thought was so scary, I was barely able to say the words. "I think McKelty was right."

"Hank," Ashley said, putting on her red baseball cap, which she had decorated with a rhinestone smiley face. "Nick McKelty hasn't been right about anything since the brontosaurus walked the Earth."

"McKelty said that he knows for sure that I'm going to have to repeat the fourth grade," I said.

"Zip, my man, the only person who knows that info for sure is Ms. Adolfopolis, the flesh-eating tyrannosaurus of the fourth grade," Frankie chimed in.

That's why Frankie is my best friend. Even at my lowest, he can make me laugh.

"Hank, you're not going to be left back," Ashley said. "You've got to relax. Do what Frankie always says. Breathe."

"Yeah," Frankie said. "Enjoy that air shooting into your lungs."

Frankie's mom, who is a yoga teacher, has taught him all about what she calls power breathing. You take a deep breath in through your nose and blow it really slowly out your mouth, letting all your worries float out into the universe. I tried taking a power breath, but halfway through it, I kind of choked. My worries did not want to go into the universe— they wanted to stay right there, somewhere between my left nostril and my throat.

"Listen, guys. I can't breathe," I whispered. "I can't eat. I can't play tetherball. I can't think about anything else until I know for sure."

Ms. Adolf was putting on her gray sweater to get ready to go out for recess duty. She stood up behind her desk and looked out at us over her gray glasses.

"What are you children doing still inside?" she asked. "Mr. Zipzer, it isn't like you to be doing extra-credit work."

Ashley poked me in the ribs.

"Go ask her," she whispered. "Or do you want me to?"

"I'll do it," I said. "It's my future."

How hard could this be? I'd just look Ms. Adolf right in the eyes and say, "I'm sure Nick McKelty was just messing with me, but I want to make sure that you're not going to make me repeat the fourth grade." It was a simple sentence in the American language, which I happen to have been speaking since I was two years old. I could do this. No problem.

I walked up to Ms. Adolf's desk. The walk from my desk to hers seemed like a hundred million miles. I looked at her and swallowed hard.

"Ms. Adolf," I began. "I have a very important question to ask you. It's about the fifth grade."

"Yes," she said. "Don't just stand there, Henry. I don't have all day."

"Am I . . ."

Suddenly, the door to our classroom flew open, and a sixth-grader rushed in.

"Ms. Adolf," he said. "They told me to come

get you immediately. Mr. Sicilian was called to Principal Love's office, so there's no teacher on playground duty."

"I'm right in the middle of something, young man," she said.

"This can't wait. Robert Upchurch got his tie caught on the seesaw, and he can't get off. He says he's getting nauseous, and he's about to toss his string cheese."

"Oh my, this *is* an emergency," Ms. Adolf said. Without even looking at me, she ran out the door.

"I can't believe it," I said, pacing back and forth in front of the desk. "Robert Upchurch screws everything up again. I'm right in the middle of the most important question of . . ."

My tongue froze mid-sentence. That's because my eyeballs landed on something that I wish they hadn't seen.

"Hey, guys, come here," I whispered. "Look at this. Ms. Adolf left her roll book out of the drawer."

This was definitely a first. Ms. Adolf keeps her roll book locked in her top drawer at all times, except when she's calling roll or entering grades. She wears the silver key to that drawer on a lanyard around her neck. It spends its entire life bouncing around her chest, like it's stuck on some icky roller-coaster ride.

I looked at the dark blue roll book sitting there on top of her desk. The answer to my fifth-grade future was calling to me from inside its cover. Just one peek inside would tell me if I was going to be a fourth-grader again, or if I could move on like all my other friends.

"Hank," Ashley whispered. "Are you thinking what I'm thinking you're thinking?"

"I think so," I answered.

"You can't do it," Ashley said.

"I'll just look at my name. Zipzer. It's the last one. I know exactly where it is. I won't let my eyes wander to anyone else's name."

"What if she comes back and sees you?" Frankie said.

"She's not coming back right away," I whispered. "She's on the playground with Robert, untying his tie."

"That's her roll book, dude," Frankie said. "She catches you with your hands on that, she's going to send you all the way back to preschool.

If you're not careful, you're going to be singing 'Wheels on the Bus' with a bunch of ankle-biters spitting up all over your Mets T-shirt."

Frankie was right, and I knew it. If Ms. Adolf caught me looking through her precious secret roll book, she would be really mad, madder even than she gets at Luke Whitman when he picks his nose and wipes his picking finger on the black-board eraser.

But on the other hand, I had to know what was in there. I just had to. It wasn't like I was just a little curious. There was a super loud voice in my head saying, *Hank, you must find out about your future.*

I looked at the roll book, then over at Ashley and Frankie. I didn't know what to do.

TEN REASONS I SHOULDN'T LOOK
IN MS. ADOLF'S ROLL BOOK

1. It's not mine.
2. I don't have her permission.
3. She's told us we can't.
4. No living fourth-grader has ever dared to look in there before.
5. I might see one of her cooties walking across the page.
6. The cootie could attack me and bite me, and I'd turn into a grumpy, gray-faced fourth-grade teacher with lint on my skirt.
7. What if Ms. Adolf set a finger trap in there that would snap onto my fingers and never come off?

8. I need all my fingers, in case one day I decide to play keyboards in a rock band.
9. Come on, Hank. Who are you kidding???? You know you're going to do it!

P.S. I know, I know. You don't have to remind me that there are only nine reasons on the list. I couldn't come up with the tenth. As soon as I do, I'll let you know. But don't hold your breath.

CHAPTER 4

Hank Zipzer D D D D D D D D!

It was like the roll book was yelling out to me.

Hank, open me! Come on. It's easy. Just lift the cover.

I reached my hand out toward its dark blue cover. This was making me plenty nervous. I knew if Ms. Adolf ever caught me, it would be curtains. I could feel sweat forming on all parts of my body—the back of my neck, my forehead, and I don't mean to gross you out, but even in the little wrinkles behind my knees.

It was really quiet in the classroom. The only sound was the big hand on the clock clicking to the next minute. I took a step forward. The rest of my life was just inside that book. I took a deep breath and reached out.

"Will you hurry up, already?" Ashley said in a loud whisper. "If you're going to do it, do it!"

Her voice scared me so much that I almost jumped out of my sneakers, which wasn't easy because they were tied tight with a double knot.

"Ashley!" I whispered back. "You scared me."

"I'm just trying to help you. Ms. Adolf could be back any minute."

I reached out again, and no sooner had I touched the roll book when I heard footsteps in the hall just outside our classroom. The door swung open, but I was able to get my hand away just in time. All three of us stood like statues, trying not to look like we were about to do something wrong.

It was Dr. Berger, the learning specialist at our school.

"Hi, Dr. B.," I said, trying to make my voice sound normal. I know her pretty well, because I work with her twice a week in her office.

"Is everything okay, Hank?" Dr. Berger asked. "You sound funny."

I wished I could tell her what was really going on—that I was afraid I was going to have to repeat the fourth grade. But when I opened my mouth, all that came out was, "Everything's fine. Terrific."

She didn't look totally convinced, but she's so

nice that she wouldn't accuse you of anything unless she knows for sure. Not like Ms. Adolf, who accuses you even when you're just *thinking* about doing something wrong.

"I was coming by to remind you that we changed our meeting times this week because of parent-teacher conferences," she said to me.

"Thanks so much, Dr. B." I said. "I'm a big fan of reminders."

She looked around the room, suddenly aware that there was no teacher in there with us.

"Are you kids on your way out to recess?" she asked.

"Oh, yes," I answered. "I'm a big fan of recess, too."

"Me too," Frankie said. "We can't get enough of recess. Isn't that right, guys?"

Ashley and I nodded like crazy.

Dr. Berger looked at us for what seemed like too long. In the silence, we heard the clock tick.

"Oh my," she said, looking at the clock. "I'm late for a meeting in Principal Love's office. I don't want to leave you here alone, but Ms. Adolf should be here any second. I just saw her on her way up from the playground."

"Great," I said. "We're big fans of Ms. Adolf too."

Dr. Berger gave me a funny look, nodded, and left. I knew I had to act fast.

"Ashley, go out in the hall and stand watch," I said.

"If you see Ms. Adolf coming, your job is to get her into a conversation so she doesn't come in here," Frankie said.

"About what?" Ashley said.

"About anything. The weather. Her gray clothes. Ask her if her underwear is gray too."

"I'm not asking her that!"

"Ash, will you just get out there now," I said. "You'll come up with something. Go!"

Ashley went out into the hall and closed the door.

"There you go, big guy," Frankie said, pointing to the roll book on the desk. "It's all yours. Hit it."

I was just about to grab it when the hall door flew open. It scared me so much that I dove under the desk—except I forgot that there's no opening on that side. I flew right into the big panel of wood that stops us from seeing Ms.

Adolf's knees when she's sitting at her desk.

"Hank, what are you doing down there?" It was Ashley at the door.

"Ashweena, rule number one about standing guard," Frankie whispered. "Keep your post."

"But I had an idea," Ashley said. "When I see Ms. Adolf coming down the hall, I'll knock three times."

"Knock four times. Knock yourself out. Just go back out there," Frankie said. I love that about Frankie. He can really take charge. And I really had a headache.

Ashley went back out into the hall, and I stood at the desk, staring at the roll book. My hands were shaking a little as I lifted the cover and flipped to the first page. It was just attendance records. Where were the grades? That's what I needed to get to.

"Could you hurry it up, Zip?" Frankie said.

"I'm a slow reader," I answered. "You know that."

I turned to the next page, and there they were. All thirty-one names in our class were listed, mine being the last. I kept my word and tried not to look at anyone else's grades. I just let my eyes roll down to the bottom of the page, where I knew my name would be.

And there, next to my name, were all my grades for the year. There were so many Ds in a row, it was hard to keep my eyes focused on following them all the way across the page. Wow, I must be the king of D-ville.

"What's it say, Zip?" Frankie asked. "Are they keeping you back?"

"I'm looking," I said.

"Looking is good, finding is better," Frankie said. "Here, let me help."

"No, I should be the only one doing this," I said, clutching the roll book right to my chest. "I don't want you to get caught."

Suddenly, we heard a crash in the hallway. It was followed by three clomps on the door.

"Is that a signal from Ashley?" I asked Frankie. It didn't sound like any knock I'd ever heard before.

Before Frankie could answer, there were three more clomps. That had to be a signal. I threw the roll book down on the desk and dashed for the door.

"Zip!" Frankie called out. "The book's open!"

It was! I turned and slid across the linoleum floor like a speed ice-skater. As I slid by the desk, I reached out and flipped the book closed, pulled myself around the corner of the desk, and headed back to the door—all in one move.

Wow, I should really think about entering the Olympics, but not right now because I'm kind of busy.

Frankie and I flew out into the hall. There was Ashley, lying on the ground in front of the door, blocking the entrance. She was holding her knee and rolling around like she was in pain. Ms. Adolf was hunched over next to her.

"Do you think you can stand up now, Ms. Wong?" she asked.

"I don't know," Ashley said. "I have a trick knee, and I can never tell when it's going to give out."

"I've never seen it go out before," said Ms. Adolf.

"That's what I'm telling you about my knee," Ashley said. "It's a tricky one."

Ashley looked over at us. I nodded at her without actually nodding my head for real. When you've been best friends with someone your whole life, you can nod without actually nodding, and they know you're nodding.

Ashley understood my signal. "I think I can try standing now," she said, letting go of her knee.

"Let me help you up, dear," Ms. Adolf said.

She reached out and took hold of Ashley's wrist. She pulled her up and leaned her against her chest, sort of tucked in under her armpit. I'm positive I saw Ashley's nose twitch as it faced the armpittal area. And to think Ashley was doing this all for me. I ask you, where are you going to find a friend like that?

"Thank you, Ms. Adolf," Ashley said. "See, my knee is much better now."

Ms. Adolf turned her attention to us.

"What are you two boys doing inside the classroom during recess?" she said.

"That's a good question, Ms. Adolf," Frankie said.

"Which is why you're a good teacher, because you ask good questions," I added.

"I'm still waiting for the answer," Ms. Adolf said. I noticed her foot start to tap like it does when she's waiting for me to answer how much twelve times seven is.

I looked over at Frankie for some help, but I saw something I had never seen before. Frankie was speechless. Wordless. Answerless. It was up to me to come up with the answer.

"Ms. Adolf," I began, not knowing where my brain was going. "We were in the classroom during recess . . . because . . . we believe . . . that you can never be too early for earth science."

"That's a very unusual attitude for you, Henry," Ms. Adolf said. She was definitely suspicious, and I knew I had to do some fast talking.

"I know it is," I said. "The old Hank wasn't that much of an earth science fan. But the new Hank can't get enough of igneous rocks. As a matter of fact, I started a collection yesterday afternoon."

I said a silent thank-you to the people who make those National Geographic specials for television. I had just seen one on volcanoes and how the lava from them produces igneous rocks.

Ms. Adolf raised an eyebrow at me. "I must say, I'm surprised by your enthusiasm but pleased."

Phew! That was close. I looked over at Frankie and Ashley. Maybe I'm getting all Ds in school, but every once in a while, I have to give my brain an A-plus.

Ordinarily, I might have taken time to enjoy the moment. But I had other things on my mind. Like what I had seen inside the roll book.

CHAPTER 5

Nick (the tick) ✓
Frankie ✓
Ashley ✓
Hank Zipzer — REDO!!!

It said: *Redo.*

That's all. Redo.

Now you know me. I'm no expert in vocabulary, but I do know a thing or two. One thing I know is what the letters *re* mean when they're in front of a word. Like take the word *rewrite*, which is always what I have to do on my compositions. It means do it again, and this time, use the dictionary.

Redo. As in not good enough. No way, Jose. Do over.

When I saw the word Redo next to my name, I knew it could only mean one thing: I was going to have to repeat the fourth grade. It was the worst moment of my life.

I thought about all my friends going on to the fifth grade, and me—stuck in the same class with my smarty-pants sister.

I thought about how Nick McKelty was going to hold this over my head forever and tell everybody he's ever met that I wasn't smart enough to get out of the fourth grade.

I thought about the look on my dad's face when they tell him that his only son, if you don't count Cheerio, is being left behind.

Wow. Redo. Isn't it amazing how four little letters can make you feel so bad?

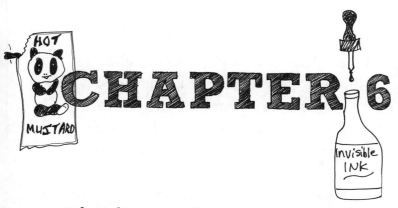

CHAPTER 6

I barely noticed anything around me on the walk home. It was like all the great sights and smells of my neighborhood didn't exist. I didn't smell the sausages cooking on Amir's cart on Columbus Avenue or hear the guy playing saxophone at the subway entrance or notice the taxis weaving in and out of the bumper to bumper traffic. As I walked home with Frankie and Ashley, all I talked about was what I saw in Ms. Adolf's roll book.

We arrived home, went directly to Ashley's apartment, and plopped ourselves down at her kitchen table. Frankie, Ashley, and I live in the same apartment building on 78th Street, and we always go to one of our apartments for a snack when we don't have an after-school activity. The only activity I had planned for that day was to worry.

"Have a fried wonton," Ashley said.

"Ash, are you crazy?" I answered. "You expect me to eat at a time like this?"

"Take one," Frankie said. "Everyone needs something crunchy when they're in a crisis."

"Oh, yeah? Says who?"

"It's basic, my man," Frankie said. "Why do you think baseball players eat sunflower seeds when they're waiting on the bench? Crunchy for crisis."

"Yeah," Ashley agreed. "My mom goes through half a bag of potato chips when she misses a *Jeopardy!* question."

"We're not talking about a game here, guys," I said, reaching for a peanut butter and jelly sandwich instead.

Ashley's grandma, who has lived with them ever since she came from China last year, had made us her special snack platter—peanut butter and jelly on Wonder bread with a side of fried wontons and hot mustard. If you've never had Chinese hot mustard, then let me just warn you that it's something you've got to be really careful with. If you eat a little too much of that stuff, the fumes go shooting up your nose, and before you know it, water comes flying out of your eyeballs—and I don't mean a few tears but more like blasts from giant-sized super squirt guns.

I swallowed the peanut butter and jelly sandwich in one gulp, without even tasting it.

"Man, are you ever grumpified," Frankie said.

"I know I'm in a bad mood," I answered, "and I have every right to be. Wouldn't you be if someone told you that you were going to spend the next year in fourth grade AGAIN?"

"You don't know if that's true for sure, Zip."

"Correction. *You* don't know for sure. *Ashley* doesn't know for sure. Her tropical fish don't know for sure. But oh, yes . . . *I* know for sure!" I hated the sound of my own voice, but I couldn't help it. I was mad.

Ashley's grandma came to the table, picked up the platter of wontons, and offered me one. She said something in Chinese, which I couldn't understand, but after she said it, Ashley burst out laughing.

"What's so funny?" I asked.

"She said if you eat something crunchy, you won't be so grumpy."

"Fine," I said. "If it makes everybody here feel better, I'll eat a wonton. In fact, I'll eat the whole plate of them."

I reached out and grabbed a wonton like an eagle swooping down to catch a fish. Without even thinking, I swirled it around in the mustard and popped the entire thing into my mouth.

"Is everybody happy now?" I said with my mouth full.

Ashley, Frankie, and Grandma Wong just stared at me.

"Not crunchy enough for you?" I said. "Great, watch this!"

I grabbed another one, dragged it through the mustard, and popped it into my mouth. I looked like a chipmunk with a wonton in each cheek.

And then the mustard kicked in and exploded like a crazed pinball inside my mouth. Up my nose, around my eyes, and into my brain it spun. Wham! Pow! I felt like all the hairs on my head were standing straight up and about to take off into space like mini-rockets. I let out a yell that was so loud it probably shattered the glass windows in Mr. Anthony's Dry Cleaners three blocks away.

"Zowee!" I shouted. "Zowee . . . wowee . . . kabowee!" Which in case you don't speak my language means, "Ouch!!!! My tongue is on fire!"

I had to do something about the flames in my mouth. After hopping around like a crazed jumping bean, I pulled my chair over to the freezer and jumped up on the chair so I was tall enough to open the freezer door. I yanked it open and stuck my head inside, flopping my burning tongue onto a carton of Mint Chip Häagen-Dazs, where it stuck like glue. Now my tongue was burning hot and cold at the same time.

Grandma Wong was shouting commands at me, but they were in Chinese, so I couldn't follow them.

"She says get some plain bread," Ashley translated.

"Tong schtuck," I answered, shaking my head at Ashley.

"Hank, I can't understand you."

I pointed to my tongue, which was stuck to the half gallon of ice cream.

"Tong schtuck!" I said even louder this time.

In case you're laughing right now, let me just ask you to try talking clearly when you have a carton of ice cream hanging off your tongue. It's not easy.

Frankie came to the freezer and picked up the Häagen-Dazs container with my tongue attached. He took us both to the sink, Mr. Häagen-Dazs and me. When we got there, he took a glass of water and poured it along the side of the container. I could feel my tongue peel off the container, little by little.

"Breathe, Zip," said Frankie. "Your tongue needs oxygen."

I took his advice and breathed deeply. Wow. Was my nose ever clear. It was so open that a 747 jet could have flown straight up into it and done back loops.

"Hank, you've got to try to calm down." Ashley gave me a comforting pat on the shoulder. "You've gotten yourself into a total twist."

"All I can think about is that parent-teacher conference," I said. "I keep seeing Ms. Adolf sitting there telling my mom and dad that I have to repeat fourth grade."

Just the thought of that scene made me feel like reaching for another fried wonton.

"Don't go there, Zip," Frankie said, putting his hand out to stop me. "Let's be reasonable about this."

"What's the worst thing that could happen?" Ashley said. "Your parents go to the teacher conference and sit down with Ms. Adolf and hear a little bad news."

"Yeah, that," I answered. "That's the worst thing that could happen."

"You can't stop it, Hank," Ashley said with a deep sigh. "It's a parent-teacher conference. Everyone has one."

"I wish I could think of some way to stop them from meeting," I said. "If my parents never meet with Ms. Adolf, they'll never know there's a problem. And then, before you know it, summer will be here, and then I'll just slide into fifth grade with everyone else."

"*Zengawii*," Frankie said. "Just like magic."

Frankie is a great magician, and zengawii is his special magic word. He uses it to make spongy rubber balls disappear or to pull scarves out of his sleeve. Boy, how I wished it would work to make my parent-teacher conference disappear.

Ashley twirled her ponytail around her finger, like she does when she's thinking.

"I have an idea," she said. "Why don't you just say: 'Hey, Mom and Dad, would you mind skipping that meeting with my teacher? Just do it for me, would you?'"

"I could ask them," I said. "It could work."

"Right, and my name is Bernice," Frankie answered.

"Come on, Frankie," Ashley said, popping a peanut butter and jelly sandwich into her mouth. "Let's put our heads into this. The three of us can think of some way to keep Hank's parents from meeting with Ms. Adolf."

"We could spray Ms. Adolf with invisible ink," I said. "Then she'd disappear, and when my parents go to the meeting, all they'd see is an empty chair."

"Okay, dude," Frankie said. "It's finally happened. You've seen one too many action cartoons."

Okay, I had to give him that. The invisible ink idea was lame. I shoved my brain into action. I stared at the window above the kitchen sink. A teapot sat on the windowsill. Ashley's family always has tea with their dinner. I like that. It feels warm and comforting.

Man, it was quiet in there.

No, it wasn't.

In the silence, I became aware that the radio was on. It had been on the whole time. We always listen to Cousin Ralphie's *Top Forty Hour* on WFUN, ninety-nine point ten on your radio dial.

And believe it or not, it was Cousin Ralphie who had the idea that was going to save my life.

"Cousin Ralphie!" I shouted, springing up from Ashley's bright red kitchen table. "I know you can't hear me, but you're the man, and I'm your biggest fan!"

CHAPTER 7

I dropped to the kitchen floor and started rolling around on Ashley's pink-and-white speckled linoleum. It's a good thing Grandma Wong had left the kitchen to watch the one show that she never misses during the day, *SpongeBob SquarePants*. I know it might seem weird for a seventy-six-year-old lady from Canton to love SpongeBob, but some things you just can't explain. SpongeBob tickles her funny bone.

"Zip, are your pants on fire, or have you just totally lost your mind?" Frankie asked.

"My mind is on fire," I answered. "Cousin Ralphie just delivered the answer to all my problems."

"I don't get it," Ashley said. "All he said was the fifteenth caller who can name ten American cities with the word *rock* in them wins a trip to Philadelphia for the opening concert of Stone Cold Rock."

"True, Ash, but you're leaving out the most important point. The date."

"May 24 and 25," Frankie said. "What's the big deal about that?"

"Frankie, my man," I said, getting up from the floor. "When exactly are the fourth-grade parent-teacher conferences?"

"This Friday. Today is Tuesday. So what's that make Friday? May . . ."

"How does the 25th sound?" I asked, grinning like a mouse that had just eaten a giant piece of Swiss cheese.

"Okay," Ashley said. "So Stone Cold Rock is opening the same time as the parent-teacher conferences. How does that help you?"

"Guess who's going to win the contest and send his parents to the opening?" I said.

"Where did Cousin Ralphie say the concert was?" Ashley asked.

"Philadelphia," I said. "And even though I'm not a geography expert, let me point out one thing: People who are in Philadelphia cannot be in New York attending a parent-teacher conference. It's a known fact."

"Zip, this plan might actually have possibilities," Frankie said. That was a big compliment coming from him, because Frankie is a plan-making genius.

"Philadelphia, City of Brotherly Love!" I hollered, drumming out a beat on Ashley's kitchen table. "Roll out the welcome mat because here come Stan and Randi Zipzer."

Ashley went into action as only she can do. When there's something that has to get done, you want Ashley Wong to be in charge. She's all business.

"What caller did Cousin Ralphie say would get a chance to win the contest?" she asked.

"I think he said the fifteenth."

She turned the radio up loud.

"That was the third caller," Cousin Ralphie announced. "Let's take a break and hear from the good folks at Gristediano's Market, where the shelves are full and that's no bull."

"We've got to move fast," Ashley said. She grabbed a piece of paper from the counter and picked up a pencil.

"I need ten cities with the word *rock* in

them," she said. "Quick."

"Little Rock, Arkansas," Frankie said.

"That's one," Ashley said, writing it down at the top of the list.

"Come on, guys," I said. "Only nine more to go."

"What about Rockville Centre, Long Island?" Ashley said.

"Excellent," I said. "Write it down. Only eight more."

My friends know that when it comes to writing things down fast, they'd better not count on me to write it down accurately. I'm not exactly Mr. Accurate.

There was a pause. I noticed that we were all being silent. I wasn't liking the silence. I looked over at Frankie.

"Name a couple more," I coaxed him.

"I'm all out, man," he said, shaking his head. "No ideas."

"Me either," Ashley said.

"There's only person we know who can spit out eight cities with the word *rock* in them, and I think we all know who I'm talking about," I announced.

I was thinking, of course, of Robert Upchurch, who hibernates in his apartment on the third floor of our building—that is, when he's not hanging out with my nerdball sister. Even though he is only a third-grader, Robert is a walking encyclopedia. That kid has so much information crammed into his bony little skull, sometimes I think he has a computer for a brain.

Frankie, Ashley, and I try to keep our distance from Robert, because he wants to be our best friend. When you least expect it, he wakes up from hibernation and attaches himself to you like a garden snail. He's that slimy, too. His nose produces more mucus than all the noses in the entire state of Louisiana. For his birthday, his mom buys him a crate of Kleenex, and he needs another crate by Christmas. He's got slightly used, super-absorbent Kleenex wadded up in every pocket of his clothes, and don't even ask what's living in the little compartments of his backpack.

Robert's best friend happens to be my sister, Emily, who doesn't seem to mind his leaky nasal faucet. That's because she is queen of the nerds herself. They both love her pet iguana,

Katherine, and can spend hours discussing the different feel of lizard skin in all four seasons.

"Dude," Frankie said. "This is a serious decision. We go get Robert, and he's going to think we want to be best friends. We'll never shake him."

"Guys, do we have a choice?" Ashley asked. "No, we don't. They're probably on the fifth caller. Let's get Robert now."

"He's in my apartment, hanging out with Emily," I said. "I'll call him."

I dialed my number. It rang four times. Then I heard my sister's voice on our answering machine.

"This is the Zipzer residence, home of Stan, Randi, Hank, Emily, and Katherine Zipzer. Please leave a message and the name of your favorite reptile at the beep."

"Hank Zipzer," I said into the phone. "And I don't have a favorite reptile. I think they're all scaly and creepy."

I hung up.

"So they're not home?" Ashley asked. "I thought you said Robert was there."

"He is," I answered. "My dad's just not

picking up the phone. He doesn't even hear it sometimes when he's in the middle of a really intense crossword puzzle."

Ashley threw on her baseball cap and bolted for the door.

"Come on, guys," she said. "No time for the elevator. We're taking the back stairs."

Ashley's apartment is on the fourth floor, and I live on the tenth. We dashed out of her apartment and ran up the six flights to my floor. When we got to my floor, I pulled my key out of my pocket, but I was so nervous, I couldn't get it in the keyhole.

"Here, give me that," Frankie said, and he grabbed the key from me and stuck it in the lock. He tried to turn it, but the lock didn't open.

"Are you sure this is the right key?" he asked.

"I'll take it from here," I said. Every lock has a little secret, and the thing about ours is that after you put the key in, you have to pull it out just a fraction of a smidge before you turn it. I did that, and the door opened.

My dad was sitting there at the dining room table. He's a computer consultant, so he works at home a lot. He likes that because he can hang out in his boxers and do crossword puzzles whenever he gets bored. He's kind of a crossword-puzzle genius, if there is such a thing.

"Hi, kids," he said, barely looking up from his newspaper. "What's the rush?" He was wearing the blue boxers with the sailboats that matched his favorite metallic blue mechanical pencil, which was stuck behind his ear.

"Hi, Dad," I called back.

I knew I didn't really have to answer his question, because he had that "I'm deep into finding a seven-letter name of a province in South Korea" expression on his face.

We whizzed down the hall and flew into my sister Emily's room, where I knew the nerd and nerdette would be hanging out. When I came flying into the room, I never expected to see what I saw. Robert and Emily were hunched over Katherine, who was lying across them both, her scaly ugly head resting in Emily's scaly, ugly lap. Robert was handing an eyedropper filled with what looked and smelled like chicken soup to Emily, who was squirting the yellow liquid into Katherine's mouth.

"Don't you guys knock?" Emily said.

"Katherine's not feeling well."

"Really? She doesn't look any worse than usual," I said.

"Hank, you have no sensitivity to the iguana world."

"Emily, it really hurts me to hear you say that," I said, clutching my heart like she was breaking it.

"Hank, this is no time for sarcasm," Ashley said.

"You're right," I said. "Ash, turn on the radio and see what caller we're up to. Robert, get your brain over here. We need it."

Ashley switched the radio from Emily's country music station (I told you she was weird) to WFUN. Cousin Ralphie was just saying that the twelfth caller had phoned.

"Great," I said. "We still have four callers left."

"Make that three, Zip," Frankie whispered. "Fifteen minus twelve is three."

Frankie knows that math and I don't party together much, and he's really nice about not embarrassing me in public. If Emily had noticed me make that mistake, I would have never heard the end of it. Emily doesn't make math mistakes or any other kind of mistakes, either. She is a Super Brain.

"Robert," I said. "We need eight cities that have the word *rock* in them, not counting Little Rock and Rockville Centre. Can you do it?"

Robert nodded.

"Of course," he said. "I can also name forty countries that produce wheat."

"This isn't show-off time, little man," Frankie said. "Stick to the basics."

Ashley was already dialing the phone. I had forgotten to write down Cousin Ralphie's number, but Ashley had it in her head. Thank goodness. It's times like these that really frustrate me. Sometimes I just don't like my brain.

"Robert," I said as Ashley dialed the last number. "Are you sure you can do this?"

"Of course I can," he said. "I can do it as sure as there are thirteen characters in the ancient Hawaiian alphabet."

"How do you fit all those facts in that pinhead of yours?" Frankie asked.

"Shhhh . . . it's ringing," Ashley said, shoving

the phone into my hand.

"Cousin Ralphie's *Top Forty Hour*," a voice said on the other end of the phone.

I couldn't believe it. It was Cousin Ralphie in my actual ear. We got through!

"Congratulations, you're the fifteenth caller!" he said. "Name ten cities with the word *rock*, and you'll be the lucky winner. On your mark. Get set. Go!"

I opened my mouth to speak, but only a tiny squeak came out. Frankie saw the panic in my eyes.

"Breathe, Zip," he said. "Oxygen is power."

I took a deep breath and tried again. I still sounded like there was a chipmunk stuck in my throat, but at least a sound came out.

"Little Rock," I yipped. "And Rockville Centre."

"That's two!" Cousin Ralphie hollered. "Eight more to go."

Ashley tapped Robert on the back. "You're on, genius," she said.

"Rockford, Nebraska," Robert whispered to me, and I repeated it into the phone.

"This kid's good," said Cousin Ralphie with a smile in his voice. "Lay on some more."

"Keep going, Robert," said Ashley.

"Blowing Rock, North Carolina. Rock Island, Illinois. Castle Rock, Colorado," Robert said as I repeated each one to Cousin Ralphie. I put my hand over the phone and whispered to Frankie, "How many is that?"

"You've got six," Cousin Ralphie answered.

We all stared at Robert. He just stared back at us.

"I'm thinking, I'm thinking," he whined in his nasal, little voice.

"How about Rock City, Alabama," Emily chimed in. "Remember, that's where I threw up clam chowder in the motel pool when we were driving to Florida."

I was pretty disgusted by the memory, but I was glad she came up with it. I repeated it to Cousin Ralphie.

"That's seven," he said. "But I hear you slowing down."

"Not me, sir," I said. "I have thousands more."

Frankie looked at me like I was crazy. Robert was squeezing his nose and closing his eyes really tight.

"Rock Springs, Wyoming," he spit out like

his face was going to explode. "And there's another Little Rock in Iowa."

I repeated those two to Cousin Ralphie. Even he was pretty impressed.

"That's nine, young man. I need one more, and you're on your way to the Stone Cold Rock opening-night concert. And did I tell you you're riding on the band's personal tour bus?"

I looked over at Robert. He looked stuck.

"Dig deep, little man," Frankie said to him. "We need you now."

Robert's whole body twisted from side to side. He looked like a baby chick hatching from an egg—you know, when they come out all wet and skinny and scraggly-looking. It felt like hours were going by.

"Time is running out," Cousin Ralphie said on the other end of the phone. "Are you still there, caller?"

Suddenly, Robert's face turned bright red. "Red Rock, Ontario," he said.

Without waiting even half a second, I repeated what he said.

"Red Rock, Ontario!" I screamed into the phone.

There was a pause.

"I'm so sorry," Cousin Ralphie began, "Red Rock, Ontario, is in Canada."

"Which is just what I was going to point out," I said, "that Red Rock, Ontario, is a lovely spot, but unfortunately it isn't the one I was going to say because we all know that Canada is not a state in the United States. It's its own Canada."

Okay, I was stalling. Wouldn't you if your whole educational future was riding on this one answer?

Robert shook his head. "I'm sorry, Hank. I'm rocked out."

I looked desperately at Ashley. She shook her head, and Frankie did too. They had nothing. It was up to me. My mind ran over every city we had mentioned. We had all kinds of rocks—a blowing rock, a red rock, a little rock. Hey, why not? I took a chance.

"Big Rock!" I guessed.

I held my breath.

"Good answer!" Cousin Ralphie called out. "What is your name, son?"

"Hank Zipzer."

"Well, pack your bags, Hank Zipzer, because you are on your way to Philadelphia."

"Actually, Cousin Ralphie, I want to give the trip to my parents, Stan and Randi Zipzer. They really deserve some quality time together."

"Your parents? Are they Stone Cold Rock fans?"

"Are they ever! My dad sings every one of their songs in the shower at least three times a week. He especially likes 'I Was a Dirt Bag 'Til I Found My Soap.'"

"He must be a real rocker, that Stan Zipzer," Cousin Ralphie said.

"Oh, yes, he is, sir," I said. "He couldn't be more of a rocker."

"Stay right where you are, kid," Cousin Ralphie said. "We're going to commercial, and when we come back, I'll tell you all about the fabulous trip you've won for your parental unit."

Just then, the door to my sister's room swung open, and my dad came in. I looked at him in his blue boxers, with the mechanical pencil stuck behind his ear. His hair was standing straight up from his head, and his newspaper was still folded to the crossword-puzzle page.

"Any of you kids know an eight-letter synonym for an extinct rodent?" he asked. "I tried pocket rat, but it doesn't fit."

That's my dad, I thought. *A real rocker.*

CHAPTER 8

I covered the phone with my hand and whispered to my dad.

"Give me a second, Dad, and we'll get you the answer you're looking for, I promise."

My dad wasn't getting the clue that I wanted him to leave.

"Robert," he said. "You're usually full of information. Any ideas?"

"Actually, Mr. Zipzer, my special knowledge is in the reptile world rather than the rodent world, although I once did a book report on the life cycle of the black-tailed prairie dog and found it quite fascinating," he replied.

"Yeah, Dad," I said, trying to edge him toward the door. "Robert's a snake-iguana kind of guy, not a mouse-rat-gerbil kind of guy."

Boy, did I want to get my dad out of there. We needed to finish the arrangements with

Cousin Ralphie, and I didn't want my dad hearing about the concert until I had the whole plan figured out. I motioned to Frankie with my eyes, but he wasn't getting it. I motioned with my head, and he still wasn't getting it.

"Hello," I whispered. "Ding-dong, anyone home?"

Frankie looked puzzled. Finally, I jerked my thumb toward the door. I gestured toward the living room, then toward my dad.

"I think you might find the word he's looking for in the living room," I said. "You know, that room out there. The one where I'm NOT talking on the phone."

"Right!" Ashley said.

"Righhhht," I said.

Frankie nodded. At last, he was with the program. He's usually good at picking stuff right up.

"Come on, Mr. Z.," he said. "Let's go into the living room. I always find that synonyms for rodents come to me a lot faster out there."

"Maybe it's because the ceilings are higher," I threw in.

"Yeah," said Frankie. "There's more oxygen

floating around. It's better for the brain."

Before my dad could answer, Frankie and Ashley had him by the arm and were escorting him back to the living room.

Robert laughed his snorty little nerd laugh, which sounds like the noise my dog, Cheerio, makes when he has a cold.

"More oxygen in the living room," he snorted. "Actually, Hank, everyone knows that the number of oxygen molecules per cubic foot varies according the density of the atmosphere, not the height of the ceiling."

"That's so interesting, Robert. I think you should go see if that theory works in your apartment. Like now."

"But what about Katherine?" he said. "She needs me."

"You're absolutely right," I agreed. "Katherine needs you . . . to leave the room. Bye-bye, little man."

I basically shoved Robert out the door, which is easy to do because his bony little self doesn't weigh much more than a pocket rat soaking wet. Come to think of it, he looks like a rat soaking wet, except without the tail.

I put the phone receiver back to my ear.

"Are you still with me, caller number fifteen?" Cousin Ralphie said. "What is your name again?"

"Hank Zipzer," I answered.

"That's a WFUN kind of name," he said. "Zippy but not zipified."

I laughed. Cousin Ralphie was always so funny and full of words. It must be amazing to have words on the tip of your tongue like that, to never have to search for a thought. Me, I'm always looking for the next word, the right word, any word. My brain isn't smooth like that. It's more like a dark, rocky cave with words and thoughts hiding behind every boulder. And I'm in there searching around without a flashlight.

"Hank Zipzer, here's what you've won for the parental unit: They'll be picked up by limousine and driven in style to Philadelphia. They'll get the red-carpet treatment backstage at the Theatre of Brotherly Love as they arrive for the Stone Cold Rock concert."

Wow. That sounded great. I wished I was going.

"At the concert, they'll be treated to front-row seats, after which they'll join the band for Philadelphia cheesesteaks, the city's most famous sandwich."

My mouth was watering. I could almost taste that cheesesteak.

"The next day, they'll ride back to New York City in luxury on the fully stocked band bus. And by the way, if they're into tattoos, we'll make a stop at our favorite tattoo artist, who will give them any design of their choice on any part of their body. How's that sound?"

"Do they have to do the tattoo part?" I asked. "My dad passes out when he has to get a flu shot at the doctor's office."

Cousin Ralphie laughed. "You're a funny dude, Hank," he said. "Real zipperific."

Cousin Ralphie took my phone number and told me someone would call later to make all the arrangements. I thanked him about a hundred and fifty-eight times. He thought I was just thanking him for winning the trip. But I was really thanking him for making it possible for me to go on to the fifth grade.

I hung up the phone and let out a big sigh of relief. For a split second, I had that wonderful floating feeling you get when all your problems are solved. But that feeling only lasted for a second. Maybe even less. Because right away I realized that problem number two was waiting for me in the living room.

There was my dad, sitting in his blue boxer shorts, chewing on his mechanical pencil, hunched over his crossword puzzle, trying to come up with a synonym for an extinct rodent.

How on Earth was I going to convince *him* that he really, really, really couldn't live without going to see a Stone Cold Rock concert?

This wasn't going to be easy.

CHAPTER 9

TEN REASONS I COULD GIVE MY DAD TO MAKE HIM WANT TO GO TO THE CONCERT

1. You could be in the Guinness Book of World Records for being the oldest person ever to attend a rock concert.

2. You could be in the Guinness Book of World Records for being the most uncool person ever to attend a rock concert.

3. You could be in the Guinness Book of World Records for being listed twice in the Guinness Book of World Records.

4. You could see a rock concert and the Liberty Bell and Benjamin Franklin's grave all on the same day.

5. You could get a tattoo of a crossword puzzle on your upper arm muscle. (Oops, he doesn't have an upper arm muscle.)

6. You could get your mojo working. (I don't know if that counts, because I have no idea what a "mojo" is.)

7. You could bring back a whole bunch of souvenirs for Emily and me. That would make you feel so good—you always say it's better to give than to receive.

8. You could have a great time. Okay, it's not likely, but the point is, it COULD happen.

9. See below.

***Hank's Note: Sorry, all I could come up with were eight reasons. So get a pencil, go up to the top of this chapter, cross out the word *ten*, and write the word *eight*. Unless this is a library book. You never write in a library book. I made that mistake once and had to spend my next three weeks' allowance replacing the book.

CHAPTER 10

I had my list, and I had my work cut out for me.

I told Ashley and Frankie to wait in my bedroom, and I marched myself into the living room. I stood in front of my dad and looked him right in the face. I told him about the concert and how I won the trip to Philadelphia for Mom and him. I told him how totally great that was, how there were people in any city in the world who would kill to have those tickets.

Then I recited all the reasons on my list of why he should go.

Correction. I didn't just recite the reasons. Nope, I acted them out like I was auditioning to star in a Spider-Man movie. With feeling. With guts. With all my heart.

My dad sat there and listened to me. He nodded thoughtfully. If you just looked at him, his head going up and down, a little smile curling up at the corner of his mouth, his chin resting calmly in his hand—you'd be 100 percent sure you were seeing a yes.

But if you opened your ears and listened, you would have heard him say one of the smallest words in the English language that goes a little something like this:

NO!

CHAPTER 11

My mom's dad is named Papa Pete, and he is not only the nicest grandpa in the world, he is one of the smartest too. Papa Pete always tells me that a "no" is just an opportunity for a "yes." So when my dad said no, that he had absolutely zero interest in going to a rock concert in Philadelphia or anywhere else in the world, I took it as an opportunity to turn that little tiny no into a big, fat yes.

"But, Dad," I said, running after him as he stomped off into the kitchen, "you've got to be open-minded to the possibilities of new adventures. Isn't that what you always tell me when I don't want to eat one of Mom's new food experiments?"

"Hank, there is a big difference between you taking a bite of your mother's meatless papaya trail-mix burgers with crushed cashews, and me standing in a stadium full of lighter-waving, leather-pants-wearing fans shaking their rumps to music without melody that gives me a headache."

"Dad, can you honestly look me square in the eye and tell me you want to miss out on all that fun?"

"Yes," he said, looking me square in the eye. "That's exactly what I'm saying. Aren't you perceptive?"

"Sometimes, Dad, you shock me, because knowing you as I do . . ."

"Hank," my dad interrupted. "I am not going to the rock concert in Philadelphia. End of discussion."

He left the room and went into the kitchen. I could hear him opening the refrigerator to get out the cranberry juice and club soda. He mixes them together to make a half-and-half, a drink that to me tastes really sour, but he says is ahh . . . so refreshing.

I turned around to see Frankie and Ashley creeping into the living room. They had obviously been standing by the door, listening.

"Okay, so that didn't work out so well," Ashley said.

"No problem," I answered. "We'll just move on to Plan B."

"You're a man of action, Zip," Frankie said. "That's what I like. Now, what is Plan B?"

"I have no idea." I shrugged. "I was hoping you had one."

"There's got to be something that's going to make him want to go to Philadelphia," Ashley said. "We just have to figure out what that is."

"My dad says people travel to see something they love," Frankie said. "Like when we went to Zimbabwe to see the village where my ancestors came from."

"And my dad went to Moscow to look at videos of small bowel function," Ashley said.

By the way, you should know that Ashley's dad is a doctor and not some kind of nutcase who loves to watch movies of people's guts in action.

"What are the things your dad loves?" Frankie said to me as he plopped down into my dad's easy chair. "Besides crossword puzzles, which we all know he loves more than cranberry juice itself."

"He loves my mom," I answered.

I sat down on the couch next to Cheerio, who was asleep on his favorite pillow. Without even waking up, he cuddled up next to me and put his head on my lap and shook his leg like he was chasing something in his dream.

"No, dude, that doesn't help us get him to Philadelphia, because your mom is here," Frankie said.

"We could kidnap her and leave a note saying that he'll find her in Philadelphia," I suggested.

"That's extreme, Zip," Frankie said. "Use your brain. What else does he love?"

"I don't know," I said.

"Well, if you don't know, who does know? You're his son."

"I'm just stupid," I snapped. "Maybe I deserve to stay back in fourth grade." I scratched Cheerio behind the ears. *Dogs are lucky,* I thought. The only thing they have to learn in school is how not to pee on the carpet. I could learn that. It's the long division I don't get.

"Guys, we don't have time for you to argue," Ashley said. "We have to keep our attention on the goal, which is to get your mom and dad to

Philadelphia. And by the way, you're not stupid, Hank."

"Bingo," said Frankie.

"Bingo. I like the sound of that! Bingo what?"

"Bingo, as in let's come up with an idea," Frankie said.

All three of us stared at one another, trying to come up with an answer to the question—what would it take to change my dad's mind?

It was so quiet, I could hear car horns honking on the street ten floors below. I heard the elevator doors opening in the hall outside our door, footsteps, then the soft slap of the doors closing. It was probably our neighbor Mrs. Fink leaving for the painting class she takes over at the senior center on Amsterdam Avenue. Every painting she does is a picture of food. Her last painting was called *Kebab: A Study of Meat on a Stick*. It showed these really juicy chunks of meat on a skewer looking all spicy and delicious, just like they are in real life when Amir grills them on his cart on the corner of 74th Street and Columbus.

"What's going on, Hank?" Ashley asked. "You look like you have a good idea."

"I was wondering if Amir is making kebabs right now. I could sure go for one," I answered.

Frankie shot me a look I knew really well, because I'd been getting it from him my whole life.

"Get with the program, Zip," he said. "We're thinking Philadelphia now, not roasted lamb."

Maybe *he* was thinking Philadelphia, but I was way, way down the roasted lamb road. Welcome to the inside of my brain. It goes where it wants, whenever it wants. There was no chance of pulling it back now.

"I have a suggestion," I said. "Why don't we move on to Plan C?"

And we did. In fact, we moved all the way to Plan M. We sat on the couch and thought. We flopped down on the living room carpet and thought. We stood in the hall and thought. We went into my bedroom and listened to the radio and thought. Every plan we came up with had something wrong with it. We just couldn't come up with the perfect magnet that would attract my dad to Philadelphia.

There it was—Philadelphia. That city where Benjamin Franklin flew his kite. Where the founding fathers wrote the Constitution. Where the Phillies and the Eagles play. And most importantly, where my parent-teacher conference was not.

Only two little, tiny, measly hours from New York. So near, and yet so far.

CHAPTER 12

Frankie and Ashley had to go back to their apartments for dinner, and by the time they left, I still had no plan. I was left with no one to help me come up with an idea. No one but my sister Emily, that is, who probably wouldn't want to help me, anyway. Besides, I don't know if you have a younger sister, but even if you don't, I think you'd agree that a person would have to be very desperate to ask his younger sister for help.

Okay, I confess. I was desperate.

While my mom was in the kitchen preparing dinner, I walked into Emily's room and flopped down on her bed like it was something I did every day.

"Get your dirty sneakers off my bedspread," she said.

That wasn't exactly the Hi-Hank-Welcome-to-My-Room kind of greeting I was hoping for, but I could make it work. Trying to be nice, I gave Katherine a smile as if I really liked her. She was crawling across the room, hissing at a pair of Emily's soccer socks. Then I picked up Emily's pillow and propped it under my head. It was stiff and made a crinkling sound when I put my head on it, not like my pillow, which is soft and fluffy.

"Your pillow feels like it's stuffed with saltine crackers," I said.

"That shows what you know," Emily said, looking up.

She was sitting at her desk, painting every fingernail in a different color nail polish. "It's filled with synthetic fibers that keep my allergies from flaring up. It's called hypoallergenic."

"Well, if you ask me, it's hypo-annoying," I said.

"Why don't you make like a tree and leaf," Emily said.

She laughed her little nerd laugh. Ordinarily, I would have pointed out that only kids in first grade think that joke is funny, but since I was about to ask a favor, I decided to laugh as if I hadn't heard that joke a hundred million times. She looked a little surprised when I held my sides and gave out an earsplitting hoot.

"You're funny, Emily," I said, crossing my fingers and toes and anything else you could possibly cross. That girl is about as funny as a cow with gas, and we all know there's nothing funny about that.

I guess Emily didn't buy my attempt to be charming, because she just stared at me and said, "What do you want, Hank?"

"I want Mom and Dad to miss my parent-teacher conference on Friday."

Emily didn't even answer me. Instead, she looked at Katherine and talked to her like she was a person and not a lower life-form.

"Get it, Kathy? Hank wants Mom and Dad to go to the concert instead of his teacher conference."

Katherine looked back at Emily and hissed. Emily took that for some kind of answer, because she went on talking to Katherine like I wasn't even in the room.

"I know, Kathy. Parent-teacher conferences are no big deal for some people. Mom and Dad went to mine last week, and my teacher told them I was getting all As and that I'm highly gifted."

I may not be highly gifted like my sister, but at least I don't have long conversations with hissing reptiles.

"Emily, I'm over here," I said. "Could you maybe talk to me, since I'm the only other *human* in the room?"

Emily put some hot pink polish on her thumbnail, held it out, and looked at it like she was Pablo Picasso. He was a famous artist who was this really cool guy, because he walked around in shorts and no shirt even when he was eighty years old. Mr. Rock, the music teacher at my school, has told me all about him.

"Mom and Dad wouldn't miss your parent-teacher conference, Hank," Emily said in her goody-goody, know-it-all voice.

"They don't know about it, Smarty-Pants," I answered. "It's not on the calendar. I moved the waxed paper *and* the aluminum foil and guess what? The whole month of May is blank. Plus, I've still got the sign-up slip in my backpack. They haven't seen it yet."

Emily blew on her fingernails to dry the polish.

"So, great," she said. "You've got a plan. Now can you leave my room?"

"There's one problem, though. Dad said no to Philadelphia."

Katherine snapped her sticky gray tongue out at me, just missing my ankle by an inch. She had made it across the room and was lying on some soccer shorts next to the bed, her snout resting on Emily's pile of lavender vocabulary flash cards. Boy, if that wasn't a cover shot for *Geek World* magazine, I didn't know what was.

"Which color polish should I put on my pinkie—the dark purple or the sparkling orange?" Emily asked me, holding up her hands to admire her manicure work.

"They're both ugly," I said.

"It's too bad you think that," Emily said, "because if you were nice to me, I was going to tell you my idea for getting Dad interested in going to the concert."

"The sparkling orange is really cute," I said without missing a beat. Hey, I told you I was a desperate man.

"Want to help me paint my toenails?" Emily said as she applied the orange polish to her pinkie finger.

"I'd rather eat raw goat," I answered.

"That's too bad," Emily said, "because I think I have the answer to your little problem, but I can only tell you if you help me with my toenails."

"Exactly how good is this plan of yours?" I growled.

Emily put her foot out and handed me a bottle of lime green nail polish.

"Paint and you'll find out." She wiggled her toes at me. I knew she didn't really want to help me—she just wanted to see me polishing her stupid toenails. Oh, boy, she had me in a corner, and she was loving it.

I grabbed the nail polish, unscrewed the top, and slopped a glob of it on her big toe. I promised myself right then and there that I would get her back for this someday.

"This nail polish looks like lizard skin," I said. Maybe Emily could make me paint her toenails green, but she couldn't make me like it.

"Robert and I love lizard skin," Emily said.

"That's the difference between you and the

rest of the human race," I pointed out. "Now what's your idea, Emily? Spill it."

"Well," Emily said, a little smile curling around her braces. "The other day, when Mom and I were at the orthodontist, they played a Stone Cold Rock song in the lobby while we were waiting for my appointment."

Emily seemed really pleased with herself, but as far as I was concerned, this piece of information was not nearly good enough for me to be painting her lizardy toenails green.

"You'd better have more than that," I said, holding the nail-polish brush up in midair.

"And guess what?" she went on. "Mom knew all the words to the song by heart. It turns out she *loves* Stone Cold Rock."

"I'm really happy for her," I said. "But I still don't see how this helps me."

"Hank, you are so thick sometimes," Emily said. "Don't you see? If we tell Mom about the concert in Philadelphia, she'll really want to go. And then Dad will have to go along with it. He won't say no to something Mom really, really wants to do."

"He said no when she wanted him to wear

those orange flip-flops to Aunt Maxine's beach party," I pointed out.

"That's different," Emily said. "The rubber thingamajiggy on the flip-flops gives him a blister between his toes. He had no choice but to say no. It's a medical problem."

"So what's your idea specifically?" I asked. I was in a big hurry to get off the topic of the blister in between my dad's toes. The thought of it was making me a little nauseous.

"Dinner's in a few minutes, right?" said Emily. "I think we should put on some music with the meal."

"As in Stone Cold Rock music?" I asked.

"Yes, oh, slow one."

"I think I see your plan," I said, determined to show her that I wasn't as slow as she thought. "Mom will really like the music, and then I can suggest one more time—in front of Dad—that they go to the concert."

"You're actually getting it." Emily smiled at Katherine, who was snuggled up there on her soccer shorts. "Pretty brilliant plan, don't you think, Kathy?"

Katherine shot her disgusting tongue out

again. This time it reached me and she actually licked my sock. I think she picked up a piece of sock lint on her tongue, because afterward, she kept flicking her tongue around like she was trying to shake something off it.

Too bad, Kathy old girl. You should keep your tongue in your snout where it belongs.

"It wouldn't kill you to say thanks for the great idea," Emily said.

That's what she thinks. I think it just might kill me.

I leaped off the bed and hurried out of Emily's room. I had to get the music all rigged up before dinner. But just as I was heading out the door, Emily called me back.

"Oh, Hank," she said. "Haven't you forgotten something?"

"No."

She waved the green nail polish around in the air.

"My toes really look so much better with two coats," she said.

"No way," I said. "And that's final."

"Think about it, Hank. What if you need my help during dinner? I'd hate to have to say no."

She had me there.

I snatched the nail polish, and as I unscrewed the top, I stuck my tongue out at Emily. Katherine stared at me with her beady eyes. I stuck my tongue out at her too.

Sisters. They'll drive you nuts. Not to mention their pet iguanas.

CHAPTER 13

My dad was setting the table while my mom was putting the finishing touches on dinner. When I walked into the dining room, I noticed that he was putting out soup spoons, and for a minute, I actually got excited. I hoped that maybe my mom had brought home some of Papa Pete's mushroom barley soup that we sell at our deli, the Crunchy Pickle. It is my absolute favorite soup.

No such luck.

"Your mother has created a new soup she's trying out on us tonight," my dad said.

These are not words you want to hear in my house. My mom is always trying to create new, healthy versions of dishes Papa Pete invented when he started the Crunchy Pickle fifty years ago. But her recipes usually taste something like cow pasture mixed in with a little cardboard.

"Please tell me the soup doesn't have cabbage in it," I begged.

One thing I've learned in my ten and three-quarter years on Earth is that cooked cabbage not only tastes disgusting on its own, it makes everything else around it taste disgusting too. It doesn't matter what the anything else is. Even if it's old leather shoes, if you boil them with cabbage, they'll taste like old leather cabbage shoes.

"It doesn't have cabbage in it," my dad smiled.

Oh, yes!

"She says it's Three B Soup," my dad said. "A mixture of beets, Brussels sprouts, and bananas all ground up together with some lima beans thrown in for texture."

Oh, no! Cement soup. You could probably hold bricks together with it.

My mom came in through the swinging door from the kitchen, carrying a big steaming bowl of the awful-smelling stuff. Her blond hair was all wild looking, like it gets when she's cooking up something new, and she had a couple chunks of lima bean clinging to her pink sweater. Even though she was pretty messy, it was really cute the way she looked so proud of her new invention. It must have been the way that scientist whose name I can't remember felt when he discovered penicillin in moldy old dishes.

"Soup's on," my mom called out. "Everyone come and get it."

Emily came galloping out of her room, carrying Katherine on her back like she was taking the lizard on some kind of crazed piggy-back ride. Katherine must have smelled the soup, because as she got closer to the table, her nostrils got really big, and she started to hiss.

"Oh, look, Kathy seems upset," Emily said. "Maybe some nice music would calm her down."

"Why don't I put on a CD?" I suggested, like I just had the best idea my brain had ever come up with.

"That's a very good idea, honey," my mom said.

Emily took her place at the table, with Katherine the Ugly still draped across her back. Then she looked over at me and winked—Emily, that is. Katherine isn't what you'd call a winker. I flashed Emily a little smile. I have to admit, the girl may be the oddball of the western world, but for once, she was really taking my side in a very cool, sisterly way.

As my mom dished the soup into four bowls and put one at each of our places, I raced into my room to get the Stone Cold Rock CD. I held it behind my back as I came into the dining room and casually strolled over to the CD player we keep on the bookshelf near the table.

"I hope you didn't pick anything too loud," my dad said. "Dinner music should be easy on the nerves."

"No problem, Dad," I answered as I slipped the disc in and cranked up the volume. I could hear the disc start to whir, gaining speed.

I slid into my chair and took a whiff of the soup. I nearly passed out.

"Smells really interesting, Mom," I said as I crumbled up a handful of crackers into the brownish-greenish-pinkish liquid. My dad was just putting the first spoonful of soup into his mouth when the music started to play Stone Cold Rock's classic hit, "Whacked Out Crazy for You."

Wang . . . dang . . . wang-a-danga . . . . . . whoop-wop . . . . . .

The bass guitar belted out a thumping beat that exploded into our dining room like a bomber diving into the soup bowl. I thought my dad was going to jump out of his skin. His spoon went flying out of his hands and sailed across the table.

Ladies and gentlemen, the soup has left the spoon.

Wang . . . dang . . . wang-a-danga . . . . . . whoop-wop . . . . . .

As the spoon flew over the table, the soup that had once been in it splattered in all directions—little clumps of it landing on the table, the walls, and my mom's pink sweater. It looked like it was raining brownish-greenish-pinkish mud.

Thunk! The spoon landed with a thud, right on the end of Katherine's hissing snout.

"Careful, Dad, Kathy has a very sensitive face!" Emily shouted.

"What about my ears?" my dad yelled back over the blasting music. "They're sensitive too."

The beat was great. Our whole dining area was thumping with the bass. Then the lead singer let out a wild shriek and launched into the first lines of the song that are so catchy you just have to sing along. Cheerio, who had been sleeping under my dad's feet, suddenly jumped out from under the table and started to spin in a circle, howling in a high, screechy voice that made him sound like a girl dog with hot feet.

I looked at my dad, and his eyes were really big like he had just seen a ghost. But he wasn't looking at Cheerio or even at the soup on the walls. He was staring at my mom.

She had jumped up out of her seat and had started to sing. And I don't mean the tra-la-la kind of singing, either. She was rocking out in a major kind of way.

And she was dancing, too. And I don't mean the hold-your-partner-and-twirl slow dance, either. All the parts of her body were shaking, and at different times.

Because I love my mom and don't want to embarrass her totally in case she ever reads this, I think I'll just describe the way she looked this way: Imagine your favorite rock song, then imagine your mom singing it at the top of her lungs. Then imagine her dancing to it with all her heart and soul. You have that picture in your mind? Good. Now multiply that times twenty. Better yet, times fifty. No, times one hundred. Okay, that's close to the way my mom was singing and dancing to "Whacked Out Crazy for You."

Let's just say it was loud and nuts and very un-mom-like.

"Come on, Stan," my mom giggled. "Get up and dance with me."

My dad didn't move. He just sat there with his mouth open so wide, I could see the silver fillings in his back teeth. My mom grabbed Emily and started to dance with her. To my surprise, Emily got into it, shaking her bony butt in a really scary kind of way.

Good old Katherine freaked out. I guess in iguana land where she comes from, they don't boogie down. When Emily started to shake her butt, Katherine hung onto her back for dear life. Finally, the shaking got too much for her lizardy self, and she dove headfirst down the back of Emily's shirt. Her back claws clutched onto Emily's shoulders, and her tail stuck straight up above Emily's head like a feather. The two of them together looked like a whacked-out version of Pocahontas doing a twenty-first century rain dance.

As I watched my mom and Emily dancing around the room, singing the words to Stone Cold Rock's "Whacked Out Crazy for You," I knew I had my dad in the palm of my hand. There was absolutely no way he could say that he wasn't going to take my mom to Philadelphia to see their concert. She was just having too much fun.

But parents are full of surprises, aren't they?

I was wrong about my dad. Totally, completely, absolutely, entirely wrong.

Even after I told my mom all about how I won the concert. Even after I played another Stone Cold Rock song. Even after I gagged down all my soup and told my mom how delicious it was. Even after all that, my dad still said he didn't want to go to Philadelphia.

"It's silly to go all the way to another city on a weekday just to see some young men who need haircuts play instruments," he said.

"But, Dad, they're Mom's favorite band," I argued.

"And here they are," he said, holding up the

CD. "All packed up inside this nice, shiny disc. She can listen to them right here in the comfort of her own home."

"Mom!" I said, turning to her. "Aren't you going to tell him how much you want to go?"

"Marriage is all about give-and-take," my mom said. "If it makes your dad uncomfortable to go, then how much fun would it be for me?"

"How much? It would be totally fun!"

"Hank," my mom said. "I'm fine not going to the concert. Why is it so important to you, anyway?"

Why? For once, the words were right there, ready.

Because I want you to miss the parent-teacher conference. Because I don't want you to know how bad I'm doing in school. Because I want to go on to the fifth grade. Because I don't want to be the only one left behind.

But I didn't say any of that.

Instead, I just shrugged my shoulders and sighed and said, "No reason."

CHAPTER 14

The next morning on the walk to school, I told Ashley and Frankie that the trip to Philadelphia was absolutely, definitely off. We were waiting outside King Pin Donuts on Columbus Avenue while Frankie's dad went in to buy us each a glazed chocolate twist. I had told Dr. Townsend that I hadn't slept much the night before because I had some worries on my mind.

"I find that a glazed chocolate twist can be a balm for the despairing soul," he said, giving me one of his extra-hard shoulder squeezes.

Dr. Townsend teaches African-American history at Columbia University, and he uses more big words in one sentence than I've used in my whole lifetime. He's really nice, though, and he has great taste in donuts.

"You mean your dad just said no, I won't

go?" Ashley asked as we continued down Columbus Avenue munching on our donuts. Ashley can untwist the braided part of the donut with her tongue without using any hands at all. She's amazing.

"Yep," I said, licking the chocolate frosting off the top of my donut, which is my preferred way to eat it.

"It's too bad there isn't a crossword-puzzle tournament there," Frankie said. "Silent Stan wouldn't be able to resist that."

Dr. Townsend dropped us off on the corner of 78th Street where our school is, and we headed down to the middle of the block where Mr. Baker, the crossing guard, was waiting for us.

"You kids are getting so big, pretty soon you'll be helping me cross the street," he said as he held up his red stop sign. "Couple more weeks, and you'll be in fifth grade. Fifth grade, Hank, I don't believe it."

Hey, you and me both, Mr. Baker.

Ms. Adolf started the day by collecting the pink sign-up slips from our parents. Luke Whitman and I were the only ones who didn't return the slip.

"I forgot," I said when Ms. Adolf asked me where mine was.

"Today is Wednesday, Henry," Ms. Adolf said, making some kind of note in her roll book. "There is only one more day before conference day."

"I'll try to remember it tomorrow," I told her, which wasn't really a lie. I would *try* to remember. And then I'd forget.

I couldn't concentrate at all that morning in class. Not that I'm the king of concentration, but this was even worse than usual. Katie Sperling was giving a report on careers and which one she was going to choose when she grew up. She said she was either going to be a makeup artist for the movies or an astronomer. Either way, she'd get to be around stars.

Luke Whitman gave his report next, and he said when he grew up, he wanted to look for frogs. Ms. Adolf told him that was not a career, so he told her he wanted to look for snails.

"That is not a career either, young man," Ms. Adolf said. Her foot was starting to tap inside her gray shoe.

"What about slugs?" Luke asked her. "Or

cockroaches? I wouldn't mind looking for cock-roaches."

"Hear me well, young man," she told him. "Picking up bugs from the ground is not a career. Do you understand?"

I felt bad for Luke. He should be able to talk to someone who really understands him, someone like Dr. Berger.

Dr. Berger! Suddenly, I realized that I had an appointment with her. I had forgotten that she had changed our meeting to Wednesday. I looked at the clock. It was only ten o'clock, and my appointment wasn't until eleven. But I felt like if I sat in my seat one more minute listening to Luke and Ms. Adolf, I'd explode. Lucky for me, Ms. Adolf was so busy being annoyed with Luke that she actually gave me a hall pass without noticing that I was an hour early for my appointment. On my way out of class, McKelty stuck his big foot into the aisle and tripped me.

"Did you have a nice trip, Hankerchief?" he said, laughing so hard that I could see his pink gums above his moldy teeth.

I didn't say anything, just gave him this smile I have that says, "I truly think you're a moron, and I'm not." Then I strutted back to my desk, stepping right smack dab on his big, size-twelve Nike that held his smelly, size-thirteen foot.

"Oowww!" he screamed. "You're stepping on my foot."

"So sorry, big guy," I said. "Your foot's so big, it's taking up the whole aisle."

Frankie high-fived me, and so did about ten other kids. Everybody loves it when McKelty gets a little taste of what he dishes out.

I headed for Dr. Berger's office. I've been working with her since the beginning of the fourth grade, when they found out that I have learning challenges. Maybe I could try talking to her about my fifth-grade future. She'd be much easier to talk to than Ms. Adolf. Come to think of it, a moon rock would be easier to talk to than Ms. Adolf.

I don't know exactly why, but I never just walk calmly into Dr. Berger's office. She says it's because being calm is not part of my personality. And maybe she's right, because as soon as I left Ms. Adolf's class, I shot down the hall and hit the stairs, taking them two at a time, even though we're not supposed to. It's a Principal

Love rule. One at a time will get you there. Two at a time will get you a visit to the nurse or worse.

Thank goodness Dr. Berger's door was wide open, because I tripped and slid into her office as if it were first base on a ball field.

"Well, hello, Hank," Mrs. Crock, the office assistant, said as she leaned over her desk to see if I was okay. "You always make a grand entrance, I must say."

"Is the doctor in?" I asked. I was pretty much out of breath.

"Breathe," Mrs. Crock suggested.

"Hey, are you friends with Frankie?" I asked. "Because you sound just like him."

Before Mrs. Crock could answer, Dr. Berger appeared at the door.

"Come in, Hank," she said. She always smiles when she sees me, which is a really special thing. It's amazing how many people don't smile at kids, like the grumpy guy who works at the video arcade around the corner from my apartment. If you even ask him for change, he frowns and says, "No change. You leave now." Personally, I think that's very bad for business.

Dr. Berger took me into her office and

gestured toward the blue plastic chair next to her desk. I sat down. I noticed that she was watching my leg as it bounced up and down like it had an engine in it. My leg has a lot of energy.

"Aren't you supposed to be in class, Hank?" she began.

"Yeah, but I couldn't concentrate."

"What's on your mind?" Dr. Berger took a sip of coffee from this mug she has that says: "Kids are people too."

Suddenly, I felt nervous about asking my question. I mean, what if I asked Dr. Berger if I was being held back and she said yes? Then what? Would I cry? That would be so embarrassing.

"I came here early because I wanted to ask a question about a friend of mine named Bernice," my mouth said, before I could stop it. "He . . . I mean she . . . has a question for you."

"Go ahead," Dr. Berger said. "What is it your . . . um . . . friend wants to know?"

This was good. I could get an answer to my question and not have to worry about being embarrassed.

"My friend is worried that he is going to be held back and have to repeat a grade," I said, trying to sound like I didn't care too much about the answer.

"He?"

"Oh . . . I mean she. *She's* worried. *She's* very worried."

"Well, I think you should tell your friend that being held back isn't necessarily the worst thing in the world," Dr. Berger said.

"Can you possibly think of anything worse?" I asked.

"Sometimes, Hank, it really is in the student's best interest. However, the good news is that it's rare that a student is made to repeat a grade. Redo, if you will."

Oh, no. Did she just say it? She did! Redo.

"Redo?" I heard myself saying. Whoa! Whose voice was that? It sounded so little and high-pitched, like something that would come out of a Cabbage Patch Kids doll.

"Redo," Dr. Berger repeated. "As in repeat a grade."

So it does mean that. It does mean my life is over.

"Hank, are you following me?" Dr. Berger asked.

"What? Yes. Yes, I am. It's just that he, I mean she . . . Bernice . . . will feel so bad. Everyone will make fun of her," I said.

"Hank, did your friend have her parent-teacher conference yet?" Dr. Berger asked.

"No, I don't think so," I answered.

"No, I didn't think so either. They are not until this Friday. If there are any big decisions to be made, they will be discussed at the conference."

I nodded. There they were again, those words. Parent-teacher conference. The three worst words in the American language—after redo, that is.

"Can I know who your friend is, Hank?" Dr. Berger put her hand on my leg to slow down the bouncing. "Maybe I can talk to her and make her feel better."

"Oh, no. I'll tell her what you said. Thank you so much, Dr. Berger."

"Tell her not to worry," Dr. Berger said. "I'm confident the school will make the decision that is best for her."

All the way back to class, I told myself not to worry. But what was waiting for me in class told me just the opposite. It told me to worry.

Big time.

CHAPTER 15

It was just an envelope. From looking at it, you wouldn't think it was any big deal—a brown envelope, that's all. Ms. Adolf was passing one out to everyone in class.

"You are to give this envelope to your parents," Ms. Adolf said as she walked up and down the aisles handing one to each student. "It contains some information that we'll need for the parent-teacher conference."

The problem was, mine wasn't a thin brown envelope like every other kid in class got. Nope, mine was a thick brown envelope, Scotch-taped closed, and about as thick as the short stack of blueberry pancakes I get at the International House of Pancakes.

Large, thick envelopes are a reason to worry. I know this because the only other kid who got the big, thick envelope was Luke Whitman. That should tell you something. Luke Whitman isn't exactly the shiniest marble in the pouch. Let me put it another way. When they're dividing you into reading groups, you don't want to get put in Luke's group. It's not a good sign.

Naturally, the first person to notice that my envelope was different was Nick McKelty. I'm telling you, that guy has some kind of built-in radar that signals him when you're feeling your lowest.

"Looks like Zippy Boy got a thick envelope," Nick the Tick smirked before I could hide the envelope in the bottom of my backpack. "You know what they say, Zippy Boy. The thicker the envelope, the thicker the kid."

Usually, I can come up with something to say that puts McKelty in his place, but I was so upset when I saw the envelope that my mind went blank. I opened my mouth, but nothing came out. It felt like there were a million cotton balls stuffed inside there. When I tried to talk, I made a noise that sounded like a cat spitting up a fur ball.

"Lay off, McKelty," Frankie said to him, trying to cover for my fur-ball problem.

"Yeah, mind your own beeswax," Ashley

added. In typical Ashley style, she squinched down and got right in his face, putting the bill of her hat next to his hairy unibrow. If he exhaled any of his toxic breath on her, she was going to get blasted into the stratosphere. But she didn't care. She's my friend through and through.

The bell rang. I was still just sitting at my desk staring at the awful brown envelope. I was sure it contained the news that I was dreading.

Attention, world. Hank Zipzer, loser of all time, is being left back.

I felt a big lump rise up in my throat, the one that comes just before you're going to cry.

I will not cry. I will not cry. I will not cry.

"Come on, let's get out of here, Zip," Frankie said.

Ashley scooped up the envelope from my desk, and Frankie grabbed my backpack. Before I knew it, Frankie had me by one arm, and Ashley had me by the other, and we were on our feet and on our way out the door.

"I got the thick envelope," I whispered to them as we shoved our way down the stairs to the first floor.

"Me too," a voice said from behind. It was Luke Whitman. "I already looked inside mine."

"You weren't supposed to do that," Ashley said to him.

"Hey, I already know they're recommending I repeat fourth grade," Luke said. "As if they need to prove it, they stuffed this envelope full of my really lousy tests and homework. But I figure I'm pretty lucky."

"Why are you lucky?" I snapped. I could feel that lump moving from my throat to the back of my eyes.

I will not cry.

"First of all, fourth-graders get a longer recess than fifth-graders," said Luke. "And recess is my favorite subject next to lunch."

Oh, great. I'm going to have to sit next to this genius all next year.

"And second of all, I'm not going to have any homework for a whole year." Luke had a big smile on his face. "I just have to change the dates on this year's homework and, you know, like I'm done. Cool, huh?"

That did it. I took off down the stairs, and I didn't stop.

Two at a time. Three at a time.

Watch me, Principal Love! I can go as fast as I want.

You can't hold me back!

When I reached the front door of the school, I pushed it open and bolted out into the fresh air. The tears were just forming on my eyeballs. Everything was all blurry, but I could make out a bright red object standing in front of the school. It looked like a giant strawberry. I ran toward it, slammed into it as hard as I could, and buried my head.

Then the tears came.

CHAPTER 16

"Hey, what's wrong, Hankie?" Papa Pete asked me, rubbing my head as I buried it in the strawberry red jogging suit he always wore to pick me up.

"It stinks," I said, wiping my tears and my runny nose on his sweatshirt. I hate to confess that I wiped my nose on his shirt, but it's true, and I wouldn't lie to you, not even when it concerns snot.

"What stinks?" Papa Pete asked. "My jogging suit? Sorry, Hankie, I just came from bowling."

"No, school stinks," I said. "Fourth grade stinks. And now I have to do it all over, and it's going to stink even more."

"Who said you have to do fourth grade over again?" Papa Pete asked, reaching into his pocket and handing me his big plaid handkerchief.

"No one . . . yet," I said. "But they're going to say that."

"But they haven't said it yet—whoever *they* are?"

"No."

"Then there's nothing to worry about. I have a rule, Hankie. If it hasn't happened, don't worry about it."

Papa Pete has a way of always making you feel better, no matter what's wrong. Last year when I cut my thumb and had to go to the emergency room to get stitches, he took the doctor's rubber glove and blew it up into a big balloon and played balloon volleyball with me in the waiting room. Since I could only use my left hand, Papa Pete did the same. How many grandfathers do you know who'd do that?

Frankie and Ashley came running out the main door, and when they saw me with Papa Pete, they dashed over to us.

"*Zengawii*, Zip," said Frankie. "You disappeared."

"Yeah, and you forgot this," Ashley said, handing me the thick brown envelope.

I hate you, brown envelope. Zengawii! *Disappear!*

"What's in there?" asked Papa Pete. He was busy giving Ashley and Frankie a big pinch on the cheek, which is his way of saying hello.

"Papers from my teacher," I answered. "Trust me, they're not going to make my dad very happy."

"I happen to have just come from your father, and I can tell you this, darling grandson," Papa Pete said, "he is at this moment a very happy man. And your darling mother, otherwise known as my darling daughter, is also a very happy girl."

"Papa Pete, Mrs. Zipzer's not a girl," Ashley giggled. "She's almost forty years old!"

"To me, she'll always be my little girl." Papa Pete flashed me a smile from under his bushy, black mustache. "Just like you, Hankie, will always be my favorite oldest grandson."

"But he's your only oldest grandson," Ashley pointed out.

"Oh, I hadn't realized that," Papa Pete said, giving my cheek a man-sized pinch.

Papa Pete was teasing Ashley, but she doesn't always get his jokes. She's not too swift on the grandparent-joke connection, since her grandma isn't much on jokes.

Papa Pete waved to Mr. Baker as we crossed the street and headed over to Columbus Avenue.

"Why are Mom and Dad in such a good mood?" I asked.

"Your father wants to tell you himself," Papa Pete said. "He asked if I'd come get you and bring you to the Crunchy Pickle. He's helping your mom and Carlos get out a big party order for Mr. and Mrs. Tallchief's anniversary party."

"Can we come?" Ashley asked.

"To the party? I don't know, let's ask the Tallchiefs. They seem like friendly people."

"I'm not talking about the Tallchiefs," Ashley laughed. "I'm asking if we can come to the Crunchy Pickle."

"Only if you'll let me buy you a black-and-white cookie," said Papa Pete.

"Deal," Frankie and Ashley both said at once.

They took off running down Columbus Avenue.

I looked at the brown envelope. I figured whatever bad news was inside that envelope was still going to be there after I ate the cookie.

I stuffed the envelope into my backpack and took off after my pals.

CHAPTER 17

When we reached the Crunchy Pickle, the whole crew was working at triple speed to get the order out for the Tallchief party. Carlos was arranging pickles and olives on a big platter. Vlady was putting fancy toothpicks in the sandwich halves, because his sandwiches are so big they need toothpicks to hold them together. My mom was spooning her high-protein, low-carbohydrate, no-taste pretend potato salad into the reusable, recyclable containers she had made especially for our deli. My dad was trying to add up the bill while looking for his glasses that were sitting on top of his head.

Papa Pete tiptoed over to the glass counter where we display the cookies and other baked goods like marble cake and chocolate éclairs. He picked out the four biggest black-and-white cookies. Then he poured himself a cup of coffee and got us each a small carton of milk from the refrigerator case. You need to have milk with your black-and-whites, so you can dunk. We sat down in the turquoise leather corner booth and had ourselves the after-school snack of your dreams.

If you're ever in a place where they have those big, round cookies that have half white frosting and half chocolate, eat one immediately. You won't be sorry.

"Hey, niños," Carlos called out as he passed our booth with the order all loaded up on his bicycle. "You clean me out of my black-and-whites. Save some for the customers."

My mom held open the heavy glass door, and Carlos jumped on his bike and rode off to make his delivery. He should work in a circus because he's got great balance. My mom let out a sigh of relief. My dad, who had a real sparkle in his eye, immediately grabbed a piece of paper from the counter and practically skipped over to our booth. He pulled up a chair from one of the neighboring tables.

"Do you know what this says, Son?" he asked me, pointing to some words he had written down on a piece of paper.

I looked at the paper, but it looked like random scribbling to me. I thought I saw an *F* at the beginning of the scribbling.

"Flipper Frisbee fork," I guessed, saying the first three words that came to my mind that started with *F*. Who knows? Maybe one of them was right.

"Hank, that doesn't make any sense," my dad said, looking at me like my brains had turned into mashed peas. Okay, so I guessed wrong.

Frankie leaned over my shoulder and glanced at the paper.

"It says Filbert Funk," he whispered to me.

"That's what I was just going to say next," I said to my dad.

"And do you know who Filbert Funk was?" my dad asked.

My dad doesn't like it when he asks a question and you say, "I don't know." He says that "I don't know" is a lazy man's answer. So I've gotten used to taking a guess when he asks me something, even if I don't know the slightest thing about the question.

"Filbert Funk was an English man who

invented funk music in November of 1974," I answered without skipping a beat.

"No, Hank," said my dad. "Filbert Funk is one of my heroes. He was the younger brother of Isaac K. Funk."

"Oh, Isaac," I said. "*He* must've been the guy who invented funk music in November of 1974."

Frankie and Ashley cracked up. Needless to say, my dad didn't. He was on a Funk Brothers roll, and he didn't want to be interrupted by a dumb joke.

"Isaac K. Funk, along with his partner, Adam Wagnalls, published *The Standard Dictionary of the English Language* in 1894," my dad explained. "It's one of everybody's favorite books."

"Except mine," I said, which was the understatement of the year.

I can't stand dictionaries. I can't sound the word out that I'm looking up, so I can never find it buried in all those dictionary pages. You try looking up a word in the dictionary if you're dyslexic like I am. The letters flip around on the page, and before you know it, there are letters floating in front of your eyes like synchronized swimmers in the Olympics. Oops, there I go again, getting off on the subject of synchronized swimmers. Sorry. It won't happen again.

"Isaac Funk's younger brother, Filbert, wrote and edited the first *Crossword Puzzle Dictionary* ever published," my dad said.

He looked so happy with that little announcement that I thought his face was going to light up and start to buzz.

"Wow, Dad," I said. And because I couldn't think of anything else to say, I said it again. "Wow."

By now, my mom had joined us in the booth. She looked very happy herself. I wondered why both my parents were so pumped up about the Funk Brothers.

"And here's the truly exciting part," my dad said. I think his voice was actually shaking. "Guess where Filbert Funk was born?"

"Blowing Rock, North Carolina," I said.

"No, Hank. Filbert was born in Philadelphia." My dad broke into a grin the size of the Brooklyn Bridge. "I just happened to read that this morning in *Crossword Puzzle Monthly*."

I wasn't sure where this conversation was going, but I had a hunch. And I liked my hunch. I liked it a lot.

"Did you say Philadelphia?" I said. "As in the place where the Stone Cold Rock concert is?"

"Yes, Hank," my dad said. "When I mentioned this little-known fact to your mother, do you know what she did? She called and arranged for us to get a private tour of Filbert Funk's home in Philadelphia. I am going to be able to sit in the very chair where he created the *Crossword Puzzle Dictionary*."

"Your father and I are going to tour the Funk House in the afternoon," my mom said. "And he said if I go with him, he'll go with me to the Stone Cold Rock concert in the evening. How's that for the give-and-take of marriage?"

She leaned over and planted a big kiss on my dad's cheek.

I could feel Frankie and Ashley kicking me under the table. I glanced over at them. Boy, did they look happy. Ashley's eyebrows were wiggling up and down over her purple glasses, a thing she does when she's trying to keep a secret. And Frankie had such a big grin on his face that his dimple popped out. It looked like a moon crater.

"So you guys are going to Philadelphia, after all?" I asked. I had to be sure. "On Cousin Ralphie's tour?"

They nodded.

"Hank, your generosity has allowed me to realize a lifetime dream," my dad said. "Imagine, my behind in Filbert Funk's favorite chair. It's pure joy, Hank. A three-letter word for happiness."

"Isn't this all so wonderful, Hank?" my mom said.

Oh, she had no idea how wonderful this was.

CHAPTER 18

Before we left the deli, Papa Pete gave me a plastic baggie full of pickles to take home. That's our favorite snack food. Sometimes we go out on the balcony of my apartment and munch on a good, crunchy dill while Papa Pete tells me funny stories about playing stickball when he was a boy growing up in New York. Those are the best times. A pickle and a laugh, you can't beat that combo. That's what Papa Pete always says, and I have to agree with him.

As I unzipped the small compartment of my backpack to put the pickles in, I noticed the pink sign-up sheet wadded up at the bottom. I smiled. I had no use for that anymore. Nope, my parents didn't need to set up a time to meet with crabby old gray-faced Ms. Adolf. They'd be in Philadelphia on Friday.

I made up a letter in my head. It was the best

head letter I had ever composed.

Dear PS 87:

We are sorry to inform you that the parents of Mr. Hank Zipzer will be unable to attend the parent-teacher conference. They have been called out of town unexpectedly. If you need to reach them, you can't. And that makes me so sad.

Ta-ta for now, and yours very truly,
Henry Daniel Zipzer

P.S. Yippee!!!!!

CHAPTER 19

At noon on Thursday, a great thing happened. My parents, Stan and Randi Zipzer, went to Philadelphia. They left us a note that said where they were going to be every minute.

At noon, they were picked up in a limo and driven to Philadelphia. At three o'clock, they'd take the tour of the Funk House. At six o'clock, they'd ride in the limo to the concert. At seven o'clock, they'd be in their front-row seats at the concert. At midnight, they'd be eating Philly cheesesteaks at Pat's. On Friday morning, they'd be treated to a tour of Philadelphia, and if they wanted, a trip to the tattoo artist. And sometime late Friday, they'd drive back to New York on the fully stocked Stone Cold Rock personal bus.

They left us their cell phone number where we could reach them in case anything came up. But believe me, I was planning to make sure that nothing came up. I wanted them out of sight, out of touch, and out of PS 87.

Papa Pete stayed with us that night, which is always so much fun. He lets Emily and me eat Eskimo Pies in our pajamas and play video games until we fall asleep. Well, he lets me play video games. Genius Girl Emily has no interest in video games. She'd rather stay up all night reading old issues of *Reptile World*. If you promise not to tell anyone, I'll let you in on a little secret: Sometimes she reads the articles aloud to Katherine, and when she does, it looks as if that leathery lizard is really listening. How weird is that?

The night went off perfectly. My parents called after the tour of the Funk House, and I have never heard my dad sound happier. He was in crossword-puzzle-dictionary heaven. They called again before the concert, and my mom said they'd try to call afterward.

They didn't, but I was glad. It meant they were having a great time. And so was I. I slept like a baby and dreamed about how great it would be to go on to fifth grade. Maybe I'd even get a nice teacher. I had heard that Ms. Warner was cool and let you watch videos on the days before vacations. And Mr. Mooser told funny jokes and didn't mind if you got a snack from your lunch bag if you were hungry in class.

In the morning, I woke up and hung around in my pajamas. It was great having no school.

"Don't you just love Parent-Teacher Conference Day?" I said to Cheerio when I woke up. He flipped over on his back so I could scratch his stomach.

"Yeah, boy," I said with a big yawn. "We have all day to hang out and do whatever we want to do."

That's what I thought, anyway.

CHAPTER 20

It was about ten o'clock in the morning, and I was sitting in my room, playing a great game of toe basketball. I was beating my own world record of eighteen baskets without leaving my desk chair.

Toe basketball is a game I invented way back in the second grade. You wad up pieces of lined loose-leaf paper and toss them all over your floor. Then you sit in your desk chair. It's better if the chair has wheels. You hold onto the bottom of the seat with your hands and scoop up the balls of paper with your toes and fling them into your wastepaper basket, which you can put anywhere you want.

I was on a hot streak. Or should I say, my toes were. Twenty-two baskets and only four misses. Sweet!

Suddenly, I heard this noise coming

from out in the hallway. There was yelling, screaming, and banging so loud I thought the roof was caving in.

I admit it. I was scared. Our building is usually really quiet except when my friends and I are making noise. But the noise we make is regular kid noise—running back and forth to each other's apartments, using the back stairs, playing ball in the courtyard outside the basement laundry room. Stuff like that.

This noise didn't sound like it was being made by kids.

I jumped up and ran out into the living room. Emily arrived at the same time, with Katherine the Ugly riding on her back as usual. Katherine was hissing and snapping her gray tongue around like it was a whip. Papa Pete was in the kitchen, baking brownies, but he came out holding his wooden spoon to see what all the commotion was.

We opened the living room door and looked into the elevator hallway. I couldn't believe my eyes. My jaw dropped so low, it nearly hit the floor.

It was my parents, none other than Stan and

Randi Zipzer. They were standing in the hallway of our apartment—swaying, singing, and tambourining, as if they were still in Philadelphia at the Stone Cold Rock concert.

My mom was wearing a black T-shirt with the band's faces on the front and the words "I'm Whacked Out Crazy for You" in hot pink on the back. She had sparkly glitter all mixed up in her hair. But it was my dad who was the most shocking.

He was wearing black leather pants, and let me just say this right now: They were tight black leather pants. My dad doesn't spend a lot of time at the gym, so those pants were tight in places where pants aren't supposed to be tight— especially the tummy area. He was wearing a black leather hat that made him look like a cross between Britney Spears and the leader of a tough motorcycle gang. And he was singing at the top of his lungs, banging a tambourine on his hip.

"Dad, where did you get those pants?" I said without losing a second.

"From Skeeter," he answered, then slapped the tambourine hard on his other hip.

The door to Mrs. Fink's apartment flew

open, and she stuck her head out. At first she looked scared, but when she saw it was just my parents, she stepped into the hall and started dancing with my dad. She was wearing her big pink bathrobe, and I guess she hadn't put her false teeth in yet, because when she smiled, she was all gums and no teeth. My dad twirled her around a few times. She looked like a big, pink polar bear I saw in a Disney cartoon once.

"Oh, did you kids have fun?" she asked my dad.

Of course we couldn't hear her over the tambourine banging, but I could read her lips through the open door. My dad didn't answer, he just grabbed onto her robe and spun her around again. She laughed, and I noticed that her gums matched her robe. I wonder if she planned it that way.

"We're home, kids," my dad shouted when the song ended.

No kidding. We would have never known unless you told us.

"Thank you, thank you, thank you, Hank," my father kept saying over and over again.

"Kids, you would not believe your father,"

my mom said as she almost skipped into our apartment. "At one point, the crowd picked him up and passed him around the audience . . . your dad!"

"But, Dad . . . I thought you didn't like rock music," Emily said.

"It's different when you see it live," my dad said, wiping some sweat off his forehead and arms. I guess those leather pants don't let a lot of cool air in. "I'm so glad you all convinced me to go. I really got my groove on."

He got his what on? Did he say "groove"? Please tell me he didn't say that.

"And the band could not have been nicer on the bus ride home," my mom said. "Turns out Skeeter, the drummer, is a crossword-puzzle whiz. And Stan the Man here challenged Skeeter—we call him Skeet—to a *New York Times* Triple Crossword contest."

"Who won?" Emily asked.

"It was a tie," my father answered as he rattled his new tambourine above his head and slammed it into his right hip again. "But I'm down with that!"

"Dad," I said, trying to clear my ears to make

sure I was hearing correctly. "Did you just say you're 'down with that?'"

"No, Hank," he answered, drumming out a beat on the coffee table. "I said I'm 'down wid dat.' Skeet says you don't pronounce the *th*. I'm down *wid dat*."

"This is the same Skeet whose pants you're wearing?"

"That's right," my dad said. "We were on the bus coming home, and I leaned over to help Skeet with a clue. I think it was thirty-nine down. Or maybe it was forty-two across. Unless it was six down. That was a tricky one."

"Dad, the pants? Remember?"

"Oh, right. Well, when I leaned over to help Skeet, wouldn't you know, I ripped my trousers right up the middle."

"It was so funny, we all cracked up," my mom said, cracking up again.

"So Skeet says to me, take my extra pants. And I did. They look pretty darn cool, don't they, son?"

Oh, boy. I have fallen into a dream that my dad has become a rock 'n' roll freak, and

I can't wake up. Someone hit the snooze button on my clock radio!

My dad strutted over to Papa Pete and danced in a circle around him, shaking his butt as much as the tight leather pants would allow him. Papa Pete laughed and shook his butt right back at him. You can't out butt-shake Papa Pete.

"Hey, Papa Pete," my dad laughed. "Let me see you shake that thang."

Let me point out that he didn't say *thing*. He said *THANG*.

My father, Stanley L. Zipzer—computer buff, mechanical-pencil collector, crossword-puzzle nut—just said, "shake that thang."

Grabbing my mom, he launched into a chorus of another Stone Cold Rock song, "Rockin' All Night in the Meadow with You," pounding the tambourine on his hip in time to the wild beat.

"Ow, that hurts," he said, rubbing his hip when he had finished the song. "I have to find a new part of my body to play this with."

Well, that did it. Emily and Papa Pete burst out laughing. And I did too.

"Hey, next time, use your butt," I offered.

We all laughed. I think I even saw Katherine's scaly lip pull back into a smile. I never knew my dad could be so much fun.

"Well," my mom said, "I hate to break up the party, but we have to hurry off now. We'll see you kids later."

"Where are you going?" I asked, the smile still on my face from watching my dad's performance.

"To school, of course," my mom said. "It's Parent-Teacher Conference Day. We have a one o'clock meeting with Ms. Adolf."

Did I just say I had a smile on my face?

Correction.

Suddenly, there was no smile on my face. It had disappeared faster than you could say, "Redo."

CHAPTER 21

My mouth went dry, and my knees started to shake.

"But, Mom," I said, "how did you know it was Parent-Teacher Conference Day?"

My mind raced. Maybe she had found the brown envelope that I had left stuffed in the bottom of my backpack under all the half-eaten granola bars. Maybe Frankie's mom had reminded her of the teacher conferences while they were doing the Downward Facing Dog or one of their other crazy positions in yoga class. Or maybe Ms. Adolf had implanted a communication device in my mom's head during Back to School Night and was sending secret messages to her. That had to be it.

"Ms. Adolf called to set up an appointment," my mom said.

What, no implant device? What was wrong

with me? Why hadn't I thought of the tele-phone?

"Apparently, there was a pink sign-up slip that a certain someone was supposed to bring home," my mom said, ruffling my hair with her hand. "And when you didn't return yours, Ms. Adolf called us directly."

My face must have turned all colors of red, green, and blue, because my mom reached out and gave me a little kiss on the cheek.

"Don't worry about it, honey. I know how things slip your mind."

"But I thought you'd be gone . . ."

"We wouldn't miss your teacher conference, Hank," my dad said. "Not even for Filbert Funk."

"Or Stone Cold Rock," my mom added.

"Your education is very important to us," my dad added. Uh-oh. He was starting to sound like himself again.

"But what about the band . . . and the fully stocked bus and everything?" was all I could manage to say.

"Oh, when we told Skeet and the boys that we had an appointment with your teacher, they didn't mind coming back to New York early," my mom said. "They said they were down with that."

Oh, no. Now she was doing it, too!

"Ms. Adolf mentioned that we should bring a large brown envelope she sent home with you," my mom said. "I assume that's stuffed in your backpack with all the other papers you always forget."

The room was starting to spin. All my plans, going down the drain in front of my eyes. Before I could move, my mom was unzipping the large compartment of my backpack and pulling out the hideous brown envelope.

I hate you, brown envelope!

"Come on, Stanley. We'd better hurry."

"Wait!" I said, desperate to stop them. "You can't go!"

"Why not, honey?"

"Because . . . because . . . well, look at Dad. He's wearing leather pants."

"So? I think they look kind of cute on him."

Cute? Maybe she temporarily lost the sight in both eyes.

"So . . . um . . . my teacher will think you're

a rock star, Dad, and then all the other teachers will swarm around you to get your autograph, and, well, you know how you feel about crowds and all."

I looked over at Emily for help. She actually looked like she felt sorry for me.

My mom picked up her purse and headed for the door. "We're looking forward to talking to your teacher, Hank. I'm sure she'll have many lovely things to say about you."

My dad gave me a soul-brother handshake.

"Keep it real, dude," he said. "Later."

And with that, he bopped out the door after my mom. As they were waiting for the elevator, I think I heard him say, "Ram dang diggety ram dang," but I can't be totally sure.

I felt sick to my stomach. I ran to the phone and called Frankie.

"Townsend here. Talk to me," he said. Frankie never just says hello.

"It's me. Bad news. They came back early."

"What happened?" Frankie asked.

"It's a long story involving leather pants and a telephone," I said. "The point is, they're on their way to school."

"I'll get Ashley," Frankie said. "We'll meet you downstairs in the clubhouse in five minutes."

Our clubhouse is a storage room in the basement of our building. It's filled to the ceiling with boxes of winter clothes and Christmas dishes and silk pillows and other weird stuff the adults in our building have collected over the years. We have a couch and a chair, and Frankie, Ashley, and I have had some really fun times there.

This definitely wasn't one of those times.

"I have to face it," I said as I stood in front of Frankie and Ashley five minutes later. "My plan has failed. I'm doomed."

"You tried your best, Zip," Frankie said.

"Here, I made this for you," Ashley said. She handed me a three-ring notebook with the word "HANK" written on the front in bright red rhinestones. "You can use it next year, no matter what grade you're in."

"Thanks, Ashweena. I'm going to miss you guys. Who will I talk to in class?"

"You can talk to me," said a nasal voice from the hallway. "I'll be in class with you."

I spun around and, sure enough, it was Robert Upchurch, my new classmate and best friend.

"It won't be so bad, Hank," the little nerd said. "We'll hang out together in the yard. I know you like to play ball, and I don't participate in physical games, but I'm sure we'll enjoy good conversations about many topics, such as penguins, the internal-combustion engine, and nanobots. I can't believe how lucky I am."

No way. I can't repeat fourth grade. Not with him. I just can't.

I'm not sure what was in my mind at that very second, but I knew that I had to get to school, had to try to stop what was going to happen to me. I ran out of the clubhouse, down the hall, up the stairs to the ground floor, and out the door of our apartment building. I ran and ran and didn't stop until I reached the door of Ms. Adolf's classroom.

CHAPTER 22

I **stood there in the upstairs hall** of PS 87 panting like a cheetah that had just chased an antelope all the way across the jungle. The door to Ms. Adolf's room was closed. A sign written in her handwriting said: "Do not disturb. Conference in progress."

I leaned up against the door and pressed my ear to it really hard. I could hear voices in there, but I couldn't make out what they were saying. I heard Dr. Berger talking. At least she was there. Her voice sounded nice and calm. Then I heard Ms. Adolf interrupt her. I could tell it was her voice, because it sounded mean like a crow or maybe a rooster with an ingrown toenail. I didn't have to hear her words to know that she wasn't paying me a lot of compliments.

Then I heard my dad's voice. He was talking louder than the others, and I was pretty sure I could understand what he was saying.

"All righty, then. I'm down with that," I heard him say.

Hey, Dad. Don't be down with that. Don't be down with anything.

I thought my ear was going to fly off my head and run into a cave and hide of embarrassment. My dad was still in his rock 'n' roll mode. Or as he would say . . . and this is very hard for me to repeat . . . he still had his groove mojoing. The only thing worse than being left back is having your dad hear about it while he's got his groove mojoing.

I hope this kind of thing never happens to you. But in case it does, I'm going to pause my story for a minute to give you a list of some things you should tell your dad never to say when he's meeting with your teacher.

Actually, he should never say these things when he's meeting with anyone.

Actually, he should never say them at all.

TEN THINGS YOU NEVER, EVER WANT TO HEAR YOUR DAD SAY WHEN HE'S TALKING WITH YOUR TEACHER (OR WITH ANYONE ELSE FOR THAT MATTER)

1. I'm down with that.
2. You rock my world.
3. Want to see me break-dance?
4. Shake that thang.
5. Let's get funky.
6. Come on, come on, come on, babe.
7. Show me some love.
8. Who's your daddy?
9. Rock on, dudes!
10. I got my mojo working.

Memorize this list and make your dad take a solemn oath that he will never say these things in your presence or around anyone you know or anyone you have ever met or may one day meet.

Okay, now we can go on with my story.

CHAPTER 23

I guess I was so busy making up the list that I missed the sound of footsteps, because when the door suddenly opened next to my ear, I was taken totally by surprise. I lost my balance, fell headfirst into the classroom, tripped over the wastebasket, stumbled across the floor, and slid on my butt right into my dad's feet.

"Who's your daddy?" my father said.

"No, Dad," I whispered. "That's number eight on the list. You have to stop saying that! Now!"

"I'll try," he said, "but don't count on it."

I looked over to see who had opened the door to the hallway. It was Principal Leland Love, the head honcho at PS 87. Oh, boy, things must have been really bad to have the principal in my parent-teacher conference.

"Hello, Principal Love, sir," I said, pulling myself to my feet.

"What are you doing lurking outside the door, young man?" he asked in his big, booming voice. Principal Love is a short man with a tall man's voice.

"I was listening, sir," I said.

"And were you invited to listen?" he asked. Principal Love has this mole on his face that's shaped like the Statue of Liberty. When he's upset, his face twitches and the Statue of Liberty mole looks like it's doing the hula. She was dancing up a storm right then.

"No, sir," I said.

"Then why were you listening?" he demanded to know.

"Because I wanted to," I answered. "After all, they're talking about me."

I know this was a disrespectful thing to say, but I figured that as long as I was going to have to repeat fourth grade, I might as well go down in flames.

"There are some things children should know," Principal Love said, "and some things they should not know. Do you understand what

I'm saying, Mr. Zipzer?"

"Not really, sir."

"Well then, I'll say it again," he said. "There are some things children should know and some things they should not know. Now do you understand?"

The truth was, I understood the words, but I really didn't know what he meant. I think if someone knows something about me, then I should know it too.

Principal Love is known for saying everything twice, but sometimes on special days, he's been known to say the same thing three times. In my state of mind, I didn't think I could survive that. So instead of arguing with him, I just nodded and said that now I understood everything clear as glass.

He left. We all listened to his rubber-soled Velcro tennis shoes squeak down the linoleum hall until we couldn't hear them anymore.

Well, there I was inside the classroom during a parent-teacher conference. Now what? I looked at the group sitting around Ms. Adolf's desk. I searched my mom's face to see any signs of bad news. She seemed tired. I looked at my dad, but he was busy looking over a stack of papers that looked like they were in my handwriting. I recognized my handwriting because it looked like it was written in Chinese except it was English.

Ms. Adolf was holding a report and making marks on it with a red pencil. She was probably correcting her own report. She can't stop correcting papers, even when they're her own. She loves that red pencil.

The only one who looked like she was interested in me was Dr. Berger. She was holding another one of her favorite coffee mugs. This one said: "Children are our future." That made me smile. She noticed and smiled back.

"Hello, Hank," she said. "Would you like to sit down?"

"Excuse me, Dr. Berger," Ms. Adolf said, "but that's against the rules. This is a parent-teacher conference, not a child-teacher conference."

"If it's all the same to you, Fanny, I think Hank made a very good point to Principal Love," Dr. Berger said. "He has a right to know what we're talking about. After all, it's his future we're discussing."

Fanny?

I had completely forgotten that Fanny was Ms. Adolf's first name. You never think of your teachers as having first names. I always just assumed that everyone calls her Ms. Adolf. Even her husband. I can hear him now:

Nighty-night, Ms. Adolf. Happy anniversary, Ms. Adolf. Give me a little kiss, Ms. Adolf.

Yuck, Hank! Stop your brain before you throw up!

Ordinarily, the "Fanny" word would have made me laugh my head off, but I was too scared to laugh. Not at a time like this. Not at a time when my whole fifth-grade life was at stake. I suddenly became aware of the fact that my heart was beating really fast, and I was starting to sweat.

Dr. Berger pulled up a chair for me, but I didn't sit down. It looked like it was tilted. I looked at Ms. Adolf's desk, and it seemed tilted too. As a matter of fact, the whole room looked like it was on an angle. I wondered how all the adults were sitting upright in their chairs and not sliding into the wall when the room was almost sideways.

"Sit down," I heard Ms. Adolf say, but, boy, did her voice sound weird. It sounded like her words were trying to push through thick, gooey maple syrup to get to my ear. Like the way the mutant moth sounded in *The Moth That Ate Toledo* just after he swallowed the potion that made him turn into his baby larva state inside the furry cocoon. In case you haven't seen *The Moth That Ate Toledo*, let me just tell you, that is the scariest part, and you may want to cover your eyes when it comes on.

Everyone was waiting for me to sit down and say something.

"If you don't mind, I'll stand," I said. My voice sounded weird to me, too, like it was coming out of a loudspeaker at Shea Stadium, where the Mets play.

What's going on with me? I was seeing funny, hearing funny, and my heart was beating a mile a minute like it does when I'm really scared on a roller coaster.

Wait a minute, Hank. That's it. You're scared. Scared of what they're about to say to you.

My father got up, pushed the chair under

me, and said, "Chill, little dude. Take a load off your soles."

Maybe that's not really my dad. Maybe my real father is still on tour with Stone Cold Rock, and this guy is from another dimension, a duplicate dad who looks like mine but isn't.

Dr. Berger was looking at me over the top of her glasses. Her glasses have lavender lenses, so you're not sure if they're sunglasses or real glasses. She says she likes them because they smooth the rough edges from the world. I don't know if that's true or not, but it sure sounds great.

"Hank," Dr. Berger said. Thank goodness her voice was starting to sound normal. I noticed I was holding my breath, waiting for the rest of her sentence to come out. I heard Frankie in my mind saying, "Breathe, Zip, breathe," but I absolutely couldn't. "Do you have something you'd like to ask us?" she said.

"Just one question," I said. "And only one."

Suddenly, it came blurting out of my mouth. I had to say it fast and get it over with.

"Am I going to be left back?" I asked.

CHAPTER 24

It seemed like forever until somebody finally said something. Why wasn't anybody answering me? It was obvious. They didn't know how to break the bad news.

"Please," I heard myself saying. "I'm begging you. Don't do it. It would be horrible. I'd be so embarrassed, I couldn't show up for school ever again. Everybody would be talking about me. Hank, the stupid loser. The moron. The kid who'll never get out of fourth grade. I really do try. I did well on that test about the Hopi Indians. Doesn't that count for anything? I'll try harder. I promise. I'll make my brain do what it doesn't want to do. Honestly."

Suddenly, I felt my mom's arms around me. Normally, I don't allow public displays of affection, but this felt awfully good.

"It's okay, honey," my mom said. "We

haven't decided to hold you back."

"You haven't?"

"Even though holding you back is not the worst idea in the world," Ms. Adolf said, "we are thinking about recommending that you go to summer school instead."

"Hank," Dr. Berger said, taking off her glasses. "We believe that for you to be successful in fifth grade, you need to strengthen your basic skills in math and reading comprehension."

She made some sense, I had to give her that. Math and reading are not exactly my strong points.

"Because of your learning challenges, if you are going to succeed in school, you are going to have to be willing to put in some extra time," Dr. Berger went on.

"Are you down with that, Hank?" my dad asked.

If it meant I could go on to the fifth grade and be with Frankie and Ashley, I'd be down with anything!

"Sure, Dad! I am so down with that, it's not even funny."

"The summer-school class is small, so you'll be able to get a lot of extra attention and individual instruction," Dr. Berger said.

"You mean, all I have to do to go into the fifth grade is go to summer school?" I asked.

Dr. Berger nodded. I felt like jumping up and down and screaming at the top of my lungs.

"Cool," I said instead. "Where do I sign up?"

Wait a minute. I'm agreeing to go to summer school?

I can't believe I just heard myself say that.

Hank, shut up before you volunteer to write an extra-credit book report on why the Japanese people like blowfish.

"We want to give you every opportunity to succeed, Hank," Dr. Berger said.

"I thought you were going to make me repeat fourth grade," I said.

"I know that both you and your friend Bernice were worried about that," Dr. Berger said. "But I want you to know that we're on your side. We are here to help you."

"But what about the brown envelope? The one that said I was going to be held back?"

"You mean this one?" my dad said,

taking the brown envelope out from under all my papers he held on his lap. "It was full of samples of your tests and homework from this year."

That's all? Then I don't hate you anymore, brown envelope!

"Your papers are full of spelling errors, Hank," my dad said, shaking his head. "Looks like you gave Ms. Adolf's red pencil a real workout. Perhaps I should give her one of my mechanical ones."

He reached into the pocket of his leather pants and pulled out a shiny silver mechanical pencil. Then he twisted it so a thin, smooth piece of lead popped up from the point. He handed it to Ms. Adolf.

"You can keep it," my dad said. "I have a whole collection of them. Would you like it, Ms. Adolf?"

Hold on to your hats for this one. Ms. Adolf actually smiled—and not that little snarky thing she does in class, but a big wide grin.

Then she said, "I'm down with that."

We all laughed.

I felt like a five-ton sack of smelly socks had been lifted off my back.

"I promise you guys that I'll work hard in summer school," I said. "I'll do all my math, and I'll read the dictionary, and I'll learn lots of new vocabulary words. In fact, I'd like to start now. How about the word *redo*? I thought that meant 'do over,' but maybe I was wrong."

"You were quite right," Ms Adolf said. "I often use the word *redo* to indicate things that I need to correct. For example, Henry, I sometimes write it in my roll book to indicate a certain report card I need to rewrite because I did a messy job on it."

"Really?" I asked. "That's why you write redo?"

"Somehow, I feel you may have run across the use of that word recently," Ms. Adolf said. "Didn't you, Henry?"

"I have to confess," I said, looking into her gray face. "I did recently run across the word."

There it was. I knew she knew I looked in her roll book. What was she going to do with that little piece of information?

"That will be another conversation, Henry, that you and I will have in private. Let me just say that it appears that you will have the opportunity to improve your reading comprehension even before summer begins. Perhaps in some after-school sessions with me, shall we say?"

I may not be smart in a lot of things, but one thing I've gotten really good at is the ability to sniff out a punishment. And to me, that sounded like detention. I'll bet you five dollars that I'm going to be getting to do that extra-credit book report on why the Japanese like blowfish way sooner that I had thought.

But, hey, at least I'm going to be in fifth grade next year.

Hank Zipzer, fifth-grader.

That sounds great.

Oh, yeah.

About the Authors

Henry Winkler is an actor, producer, and director, and he speaks publicly all over the world. In addition, he has a star on Hollywood Boulevard, was presented with the order of the British Empire by the Queen of England, and the jacket he wore as the Fonz hangs in the Smithsonian Museum in Washington, DC. But if you asked him what he was proudest of, he would say, "Writing the Hank Zipzer books with my partner, Lin Oliver." He lives in Los Angeles with his wife, Stacey. They have three children named Jed, Zoe, and Max, and two dogs named Monty and Charlotte. Charlotte catches a ball so well that she could definitely play outfield for the New York Mets.

Lin Oliver is a writer and producer of movies, books, and television series for children and families. She has written more than twenty-five novels for children, and one hundred episodes of television. She is cofounder and executive director of the Society of Children's Book Writers and Illustrators, an international organization of twenty thousand authors and illustrators of children's books. She lives in Los Angeles with her husband, Alan. They have three sons named Theo, Ollie, and Cole. She loves tuna melts, curious kids, any sport that involves a racket, and children's book writers everywhere.